The Widower

AMISH COUNTRY BRIDES

Jennifer Spredemann

© 2021

Published in Indiana by *Blessed Publishing*.

www.jenniferspredemann.com

All Scripture quotations are taken from the *King James Version* of the *Holy Bible*.

Cover design by *iCreate Designs* ©

ISBN: 978-1-940492-58-2
10 9 8 7 6 5 4 3 2 1

Get a FREE short story as my thank you gift to you when you sign up for my newsletter here:
www.jenniferspredemann.com

BOOKS by JENNIFER SPREDEMANN

Learning to Love – Saul's Story
(Sequel to Chloe's Revelation)

AMISH BY ACCIDENT TRILOGY
Amish by Accident
*Englisch on Purpose (*Prequel to *Amish by Accident)*
*Christmas in Paradise (*Sequel to *Amish by
Accident)* (co-authored with Brandi Gabriel)

AMISH SECRETS SERIES
An Unforgivable Secret - Amish Secrets 1
A Secret Encounter - Amish Secrets 2
A Secret of the Heart - Amish Secrets 3
An Undeniable Secret - Amish Secrets 4
A Secret Sacrifice - Amish Secrets 5 (co-authored
with Brandi Gabriel)
A Secret of the Soul - Amish Secrets 6
A Secret Christmas – Amish Secrets 2.5 (co-authored
with Brandi Gabriel)

AMISH BIBLE ROMANCES
An Amish Reward (Isaac)
An Amish Deception (Jacob)
An Amish Honor (Joseph)
An Amish Blessing (Ruth)
An Amish Betrayal (David)

BOOKS by J.E.B. SPREDEMANN
AMISH GIRLS SERIES

Joanna's Struggle
Danika's Journey
Chloe's Revelation
Susanna's Surprise
Annie's Decision
Abigail's Triumph
Brooke's Quest
Leah's Legacy
A Christmas of Mercy – Amish Girls Holiday

Unofficial Glossary
of Pennsylvania Dutch Words

Ach – Oh

Bensel – Silly/Silly child

Boppli/Bopplin – Baby/Babies

Bruder/Brieder – Brother/Brothers

Bu/Buwe – Boy/Boys

Chust – Just

Daed/Dat – Dad

Dawdi – Grandfather

Dawdi haus – A small dwelling typically used for grandparents

Denki – Thanks

Der Herr – The Lord

Dummkopp – Dummy

Englischer – A non-Amish person

Fraa – Wife

G'may – Members of an Amish fellowship

Gott – God

Gross sohn – Grandson

Gut – Good

Jah – Yes

Kapp – Amish head covering

Kinner – Children

Kumm – Come

Maed/Maedel – Girls/Girl

Mamm – Mom

Rumspringa – Running around period for Amish youth

Schatzi – Sweetheart

Schweschder(n) – Sister(s)

Sohn – Son

Wunderbaar – Wonderful

Author's Note

The Amish/Mennonite people and their communities differ one from another. There are, in fact, no two Amish communities exactly alike. It is this premise on which this book is written. I have taken cautious steps to assure the authenticity of Amish practices and customs. Old Order Amish and New Order Amish may be portrayed in this work of fiction and may differ from some communities. Although the book may be set in a certain locality, the practices featured in the book may not necessarily reflect that particular district's beliefs or culture. This book is purely fictional and built around a fictional community, even though you may see similarities to real-life people, practices, and occurrences.

We, as *Englischers*, can learn a lot from the Plain People and their simple way of life. Their hard work, close-knit family life, and concern for others are to be applauded. As the Lord wills, may this special culture continue to be respected and remain so for many centuries to come, and may the light of God's salvation reach their hearts.

ONE

Titus Troyer raced forward with his shopping cart, hoping to catch a glimpse of the pretty young Amish woman he'd just seen in the previous aisle. If he timed it right, she'd be passing by the moment he reached the end cap.

"Why are you walking so fast, *Daed*?" His daughter's small voice snapped his attention back to his children. "You forgot the noodles."

"We'll come back for them," he assured.

"But they're right there." She tugged at his shirt and gestured behind them.

"Chust wait, *dochder*. I thought I saw somebody we knew." At this moment, though, he couldn't remember who the young woman was. He knew she was part of the *g'may*, but he also realized he hadn't attended school with her. Yet, something about her seemed quite familiar.

He'd probably know if he paid more attention to the women's side during church. He was usually too busy trying to keep his own *kinner* in line, though, and attempting to pay attention to the preachers. When he did occasionally glance toward the female sector, he was searching for his *mamm* and *dochder*. Moreover, he couldn't abide the heartache of knowing he'd never see his *fraa* sitting amongst the women again. It had taken him months just to lift his eyes in that direction.

He moved closer to the end aisle with the *kinner*.

And then the young woman he'd been eyeing passed by.

"Look, *Daed.* There goes Teacher Martha's *schweschder.*"

Ach, so that's who she was!

He frowned. Just his luck. She *would* have to be related to Martha Miller—*nee*, Martha Beachy now. The woman he had hoped to court and marry. That had ended in disaster. If he'd only known she had her eye on Jaden Beachy, he wouldn't have attempted to pursue her. *Ach*, but he'd felt like a fool. Now, the couple was married and had twin *bopplin*.

He'd thought Martha had been perfect for him and the *kinner*. He'd been terribly wrong.

Jah, he'd made a *dummkopp* out of himself for sure.

"Let's go say hello," his daughter urged.

"*Nee.*" As much as he wanted to, he wouldn't dare. Who knew what she thought of the silly widower who had tried to steal her sister away from her now-husband? His face heated thinking of the time both he and Jaden had come to call on Martha on the same day. *Ugh.*

"Let's finish up our shopping. The driver is waiting."

Although their Amish community wasn't that far from town, he opted to hire a driver instead of taking the horse and buggy out onto the busy highway. There had already been too many accidents on that stretch of road.

Like the one that had claimed his sweet *fraa's* life.

Sorrow seized his heart once again as the memories of that fateful day two years, three months, and five days ago washed over him. Helen had stopped at the stop sign, then pulled the buggy onto the highway just to cross over. Apparently, she hadn't seen or heard the vehicle approaching on that foggy morning. And the *Englisch* driver hadn't seen her until it was too late. Titus had been in the barn tending to his chores when he heard the tires screech. In that moment, he'd known it was his beloved.

And his world was forever changed.

No more coming in from morning chores to hear her bustling in the kitchen, while delicious aromas tantalized his senses. No more hearing her sing-song voice floating through the air as she read silly children's books to the *kinner*. No more of just the two of them relaxing by the fire after the *kinner* had gone to bed. No more sharing their hopes, their dreams, their love...

All of it had been snatched from him in an instant.

She had been there one moment, then gone the next. No time to prepare his *kinner*. No time to prepare his heart. And her loss had cut him deeply.

He'd be lying if he said he hadn't been angry at *Der Herr*. Or that he understood or agreed with Him. Because he didn't. As far as he could see, there was no *gut* reason to cut Helen's life short. Not one.

But he did understand that *Gott* was sovereign and He had a plan that Titus knew nothing about. Knowing that fact didn't eradicate the pain, though.

Nee, it lingered. Still.

Before Helen passed, Titus's trips to the grocery store had been minimal. Now, they were almost a weekly occurrence. He didn't really care to use the self-checkout registers, but sometimes the other lanes had

4

long lines. Since he had the *kinner* in tow, fastest was best.

As he rang up the groceries, a Plain older man—from another Amish district, he guessed—made faces at his youngest *kinner*. The children laughed in return.

Titus finished up, snatched his receipt from the machine, then waved to the older man before heading out the door to find his driver. Once outside, he located the vehicle, but saw that it was unattended, which meant they were locked out.

He sighed, then guided the children to the nearest outdoor bench.

"Waiting for your driver too?" It was the older man from inside the store.

"*Jah*. We finished up our shopping early."

"*Chust* three *kinner*?"

"*Jah*."

"I don't ever recall shopping on my own with the little ones." The man stroked his hoary beard.

"My *fraa* used to do it, but…" Titus let his voice trail off.

"*Mamm* is *dot*," his oldest, Rose, volunteered.

"I see." The man nodded as his lips turned downward. "Lost my *fraa* too. It's a tough road. How long has she been gone?"

"Two years, about."

The man extended his hand. "Name's Sammy Eicher." His smile lit up his entire countenance.

"Titus Troyer." He shook the older man's hand.

"I'm from Detweiler's district."

Same as Martha now. Which, fortunately, meant he didn't have to see her and her husband, Jaden, at meeting every other Sunday. However, if he found the courage to get to know her *schweschder*, he might be seeing the young couple more often.

"We're from Bontrager's."

"I have many friends there." Sammy's grin widened, then he stroked his beard again. "You wouldn't happen to be interested in meeting up with me and my friends?"

Titus shook his head. "I appreciate the offer, but I've got my *kinner*. And not to mention work and whatnot." He probably shouldn't have mentioned work, since he hadn't been back since Helen died. Was that being dishonest?

"I see." Sammy dug into his pocket, then pulled a pen from his shirt. "If you change your mind, this is the number to my phone shanty. You need something, *chust* call." He handed Titus a receipt with a number scrawled on the back.

"That's nice of you. *Denki*." He tucked the paper into his pocket.

"My *gross sohn* and his family live with me. I'm sure the *kinner* would love new friends," Sammy said.

"I thought Detweiler's group disfellowshipped with Bontrager's."

"I suppose they did. Not me." He winked. "All are welcome at the Eicher place."

"I appreciate that."

"Men need other men for encouragement. Especially in this day and age. I have a feeling it was *Der Herr* who planned for our paths to cross today."

Titus nodded. "Quite possible." Their driver pulled up and he nudged the *kinner* to stand from the bench. "Well, we best be going. It was *gut* to meet you."

"*Gut* to meet you too." Sammy waved at the *kinner* as they loaded into the minivan.

TWO

*E*mily Miller clutched one of the four tiny kittens in her hand as its minute meow intensified. She stroked its fur in an attempt to calm it, filled the small syringe with a diluted milk mixture, then commenced feeding the poor motherless *boppli*.

They'd found Flash, the kittens' *mamm*, out on the road dead just yesterday. Flash had earned her name due to her lightning speed. As an abandoned kitten, she'd obviously been a house cat. When the Millers took her in, it was agreed that the feline would be an outside dweller, as were all their animals. But that fact hadn't discouraged Flash from attempting to dash into the house at every opportunity. Flash eventually learned her place and found joy in hunting moles and mice on the farm. Which was probably the activity she'd been engaged in on that fateful night when she'd lost her life.

Since the kittens were only two weeks old, they'd need to be bottle fed until they could eat on their own. This one, the crier, was a light calico color like her momma had been. When Flash had the kittens, they were nowhere to be found, even after an extensive search of the farm. They'd figured she gone off to birth them, since she'd abandoned her usual plush bed on the porch. Fortunately, Nathaniel had found them in a secluded corner of the barn loft, nestled between two bales of hay. If he hadn't found them, the poor creatures wouldn't have survived on their own.

Emily once again whispered a prayer of thanksgiving to *Der Herr* for leading Nathaniel to the helpless creatures.

Once the last kitten was satisfied, she showered a little attention on each of them, then returned them to their box in the mudroom. They still begged for attention, but they'd be settled and asleep in a few minutes.

As she dried her clean hands, she glanced out the window and noticed a buggy pulling up to her roadside produce stand. She'd go to greet whoever it was and thank them for stopping by. When she wasn't too busy with other chores, she enjoyed sitting out at the stand, reading a book, rearranging her goods, and conversing with the customers. She'd met many interesting people that way, and sometimes got to peer into *Englischers'* lives.

"Hello," she called out her greeting before even seeing who it was.

"See, *Dat*? It's Teacher Martha's *schweschder*." A young female voice said as Emily rounded the corner.

It wasn't the first time she'd been referred to as Teacher Martha's sister, although her older sister Martha hadn't taught at the schoolhouse in over a year now. Once Martha and Jaden Beachy had gotten hitched and had their twin babies, they'd relocated to Bishop Detweiler's neighboring district where Jaden taught school. No doubt their *kinner* would grow up smart, or at least to be book lovers, since both of their parents were teachers.

"Hello." Titus Troyer, the widower, nodded. He held a youngster by the hand, while the other children—a boy about five, and the girl who must be at least seven, if she'd been in Martha's class last year— perused the items on the shelves. "I hope we didn't interrupt your work."

"*Nee*, not at all. I just finished feeding our kittens." Emily smiled.

The young girl's face lit up at the mention of the kittens. "I love kittens."

"Would you like to see them? That is, if it's okay with your *dat*." She eyed Titus.

"I wanna see 'em too!" the middle boy said.

"Well, then, it looks like you better show us those kittens." Titus grinned.

"Okay. They're just inside the mudroom." She began walking up the driveway toward the house. "I'm Emily, by the way. I don't think we've ever *officially* met."

Something sparked in his eye. Surprise, maybe? "I'm Titus. *Gut* to meet you, Emily."

He seemed a little nervous, and she wanted to put him at ease. "You went to school with *mei bruder* Paul and *schweschder* Martha, right?"

"*Jah*."

"And you're related to Amy Troyer, ain't so?"

"We're first cousins."

Emily nodded. "I started school when Martha finished. When did you finish?"

"The year before your *schweschder*, I think."

"So that would make you..."

"Old." He laughed.

"*Nee*, not too old." She flicked a glance in his direction and they shared a smile. She was glad she'd set his mind at ease. "About thirty-four?"

He nodded.

"I'm twenty-four."

A timid smile formed. "Not too young."

She stepped into the mudroom, and held the door open for their small crew to enter. "Just a minute. I'm going to let *Mamm* know what's going on."

"Alright," Titus said.

She stepped into the kitchen, then closed the door behind her. "*Mamm*, Titus Troyer and his *kinner* are here. I'm showing them the kittens."

"That's fine, *dochder*. Do you want to invite them for supper?" *Mamm* asked.

Emily chewed on her lip, then glanced at the closed mudroom door. "I don't think so. He might get the wrong impression." *Although*...what would it be like to have them over for supper?

"No harm in inviting a widower for a meal."

"I know, and I'd like to. It's just, now's not the right time." She'd like to feel more comfortable with them before doing something like that.

"Whatever you say, *dochder*."

She snatched a small container of milk and her feeding syringe to show the children. "I need to go back out there. The *kinner* are excited to see the kittens."

Emily stepped back into the mudroom. "*Ach*, sorry. That took longer than I thought it would."

"I hear them crying," the middle boy said.

A lone cry sounded from the laundry basket she'd been keeping them contained in. Soon, she'd need to find something larger to house them. They'd already outgrown the banana box they'd first been in. "*Jah*. That's probably Cali. She's the most dramatic of the bunch. She probably heard you talking. Any time she knows someone is near, she begs for attention."

She lifted the towel she'd placed over the top of the basket, which resulted in a chorus of all four kittens mewing. "*Kumm*, now. Someone wants to meet you," she addressed the kittens in a soft voice.

She gestured toward the wooden bench *Dat* had made specifically for the mudroom. They typically used the bench to put their boots on or remove them. "If you have a seat, I'll let you hold them," she told the children.

Titus nodded for them to sit. Excitement danced in the children's eyes as they took a seat on the bench. Titus helped the youngest one up.

"Now, you have to be careful because their little claws are very sharp. They don't have a *mamm* anymore, so they'll think you're their *mamm*." She handed each one a kitten, and kept one for herself. Titus assisted the youngest boy.

"We don't have no *mamm*, neither," the older boy said.

14

Ach, she should have thought before she'd spoken.

"I know. I'm sorry." As she met Titus's gaze, the pain in his eyes was nearly her undoing. *Ach*, she couldn't imagine his heartache. Their heartache. Her chin quivered unbidden, but she blinked back her tears. No need to make the *kinner* sad. "Maybe your *mamm* is taking care of the kitties' *mamm* in Heaven," she attempted a cheerful tone.

"*Nee*," the girl said. "Berry Ted said animals don't go to Heaven."

"Well, I don't know about that," Emily said. "Because the Bible talks about animals in Heaven."

"It does?" The boy's attention was riveted on her.

She nodded. "Sure does. *Dat* was just reading about it last night. Jesus is going to come back on a white horse."

"I've got a pony," the boy said.

"I bet it's fun. You know..." She tapped her chin. "You never told me your names."

"I'm Rose. *Mamm* named me after her favorite flower," the girl volunteered, her cheeks blushing slightly like her father's.

"That's a very pretty name, and a pretty flower," Emily smiled, glancing briefly at Titus.

"Is it your favorite too?" Was there expectation in Rose's eyes?

Emily shrugged. "I think it's too hard to pick a favorite flower. They're all so lovely. I do love the way roses smell, though."

Rose smiled. "Me, too."

"She don't smell like no rose, though," her younger brother said. "She smells like the fancy peach spray *Dat* bought her."

"Peaches smell great, too." Emily studied the boy. "What's your name?"

"Titus, like my *dat*. But they call me Ty."

"I think Ty's a fine name too. It's *gut* to be named after a nice man like your *dat*." She allowed herself to examine Titus, and noticed a hint of a smile on his lips. He stroked a kitten with the youngest one, whose name she hadn't gotten yet. "And who is this?"

"This is Benuel," Titus said.

"Nice to meet you, Benuel." She stroked the kitten she held. "And how old are you?" she asked the boy in Pennsylvania Dutch.

He held up three fingers.

"I remember when I was three." The joyful memory warmed her heart and escaped in a smile. "That was when I first got to pet a cat. It was love at first sight."

At the words, Titus momentarily caught and held her gaze. *Ach*, had she ever seen such attractive hazel eyes?

"I'm five," Ty's words distracted her. "And my sister's seven."

"You'll probably be going to school before too long, ain't so? I bet you're excited."

Ty nodded. "We live on the same road as the school. It ain't too far."

The kitten in Emily's arms began meowing. She held up the syringe and showed it to the *kinner*. "See this? This is how I feed them." She dipped the syringe into a jar of warm milk and filled it, then placed the syringe in the kitten's mouth.

"That's neat!" Ty laughed.

"Would you like to try? They've already eaten, but I'm sure your kitten would love a little extra milk." She filled the syringe and handed it to Titus. His fingers brushing hers in the exchange did something funny to her insides. *Ach.* "Just be careful not to push it in too fast or the kitty will choke."

"Okay." Ty's reply held solemnity.

"Can my kitty have some too?" Rose asked.

"Sure. Just as soon as Ty's done."

"If you're interested," Titus said, "I've got some old nursing bottles at the house that we used for our kittens some years back. I think the rubber's still *gut*. You're welcome to them."

"*Ach*, that would be *wunderbaar. Denki.*" She

smiled. "I'm sure a bottle would feel a lot more natural for them than the syringe."

Titus nodded. "I could drop them by tomorrow, if you'd like."

"That's very kind of you, Titus."

"It's no problem. It would be my pleasure."

Something about the way he said the words warmed Emily from the inside out. They'd almost felt like a caress. But that was silly, wasn't it?

Surely, she'd just been imagining his voice dipping low. Surely, she'd just been imagining their gazes connecting. Surely, she'd just been imagining the jolt of excitement when their hands touched.

Or had she?

THREE

The moment Emily Miller walked up to the produce stand, Titus completely forgot what he'd come for. *Nee*, the beautiful *maedel* had swept him—and apparently his *kinner*—right off their feet!

"Lovely" could not even begin to describe her. She was friendly, kind, gentle, and easy on the eyes, to his thinking. The kind of *maedel* that would make a *wunderbaar mamm* and *fraa*.

But Titus had no clue how to figure out whether she was interested in him or not. Surely, she was simply being nice. For all he knew, she had young men with buggies lined up, waiting to court her. Why on earth would she be interested in someone like him, who'd already been hitched once and had three *kinner* to raise? Not to mention that he was ten years her senior.

She hadn't refused his offer of the cat bottles, so that was *gut*. But why would she? Bottles had nothing to do with relationships. So, he'd deliver the bottles tomorrow. Then what? Invite her to supper? *Nee*, he wasn't that great of a cook. That might turn her off for sure.

Think, Titus! What excuse could he use to see her again? He couldn't stop at her produce stand every day. That would just be awkward.

"What would you like?" Emily stood there patiently waiting for his answer.

A date with you. He gave his head a slight shake. "What do you suggest?"

"Well, the tomatoes are nice and sweet."

"Okay, I'll take a basket."

"But, *Dat*, you hate tomatoes," Ty reminded him.

He ruffled the little guy's hair. "*Ach, jah.*" His face was turning hot now. "Uh, we'll give them to your *grossmammi*. She'll make something *gut* with them."

"The strawberries are popular right now, too. These are the first of the season." Emily suggested. "They taste *wunderbaar* in a strawberry shortcake."

"I'm afraid I have no clue how to make strawberry shortcake." Titus chuckled.

"I could make you some."

Emily Miller is offering to make me strawberry shortcake? Ach.

Emily Miller was offering to make him strawberry shortcake. Had he heard her right? Or maybe he was daydreaming. He coughed, as he fought for words. "I'd like that."

"I love strawberries, *Dat*. Let's get a lot." Rose's smile stretched across her face.

"Strawberry shortcake really isn't that difficult. Maybe I could...I mean, if you'd like...I could teach Rose how to make it."

Titus pictured Emily standing in his kitchen barefoot with tendrils of her chestnut hair peeking out under a kerchief, and his heart raced frantically. He couldn't speak, so he simply nodded.

"Really, *Dat*?" Rose giggled. "That would be *wunderbaar*!"

Ach, when had his *dochder* been this excited about something?

"I want some too," Ty said.

Emily's smile lit up her entire mien. "Rose and I would make enough for everyone, Ty." She tweaked his cheek. "Including you."

"Can you come today?" Ty clapped his hands.

Today? Titus gulped. Panic began to set in. *Nee*, not today. The house was...well, it wasn't a complete disaster, but it certainly wasn't ready for the likes of Emily Miller.

"It's up to your *dat*." Emily turned her eyes on him.

"Would tomorrow work?" He recovered. "I…I could pick you up when I come by to drop off the bottles for the kittens." Although, the thought of Emily sitting next to him in his buggy caused his hands to perspire.

"Oh." Her fingertips tapped on her lips, drawing his attention to them. He quickly looked away. No need to be pondering Emily Miller's lips. "That would be great," she said.

"It would?" *It's not a date*, he reminded himself.

"*Jah*. I mean, I'd have to enlist one of my siblings for kitten duty."

Which meant she was planning to be gone from the house for a while. With him. In his buggy. At his home. With his *kinner*. Sharing food. *Ach*, it sounded heavenly.

"You're sure?" Because he wasn't sure *any* of this conversation was actually taking place.

"*Jah*. It will be fun." She winked at Rose.

He pulled out his wallet and grasped a twenty-dollar bill. "Is this enough for the strawberries and tomatoes?"

"More than enough."

"*Gut*. Keep the change." He smiled.

"*Denki*." She lightly touched his shirt sleeve, the

softness of her fingers seeping through to his skin. "And go ahead and let the *kinner* eat those strawberries. I'll bring fresh ones tomorrow."

As Titus and the *kinner* traveled home, he *still* wondered if he wasn't dreaming this day up. When he awoke this morning, the thought that Martha Miller's little *schweschder* would be gracing them with her presence the following evening would have never even crossed his mind. Never in a million years.

But sometimes life held surprises. Some *gut*, some bad. He just so happened to like this surprise. A lot.

He took a calming breath and basked in the wonder of *Der Herr's* goodness. *"Denki, Gott,"* he whispered.

FOUR

*E*mily quickly checked the time. *Jah*, her *bruder's* store would still be open.

Hopefully, her best friend, Bailey, was working there today because she really needed to talk to her. Since her friend married Timothy Stoltzfoos and had a *boppli*, they hadn't spent as much time together as they used to. Emily missed those days, but she understood the demands of a husband and *boppli*.

Someday, she hoped to find herself in the same predicament.

Titus's shy smile flashed in her mind's eye, causing butterflies to dance in her belly. Could Titus be the one *Der Herr* had planned for her? She'd never considered a relationship with a widower. But the more she thought about it, the more the idea appealed to her. She'd already fallen in love with his *kinner*. She couldn't imagine that falling in love with their *dat* would take much effort on her part.

But how did *he* feel about her?

"Was that Titus Troyer and his *kinner* I just saw driving off?" A voice distracted her and she turned to see her oldest sister.

"*Ach*, Martha. When did you get here?"

"Just now." Her sister smiled, holding a *boppli* in her arms.

"And I was just about to leave." Emily pouted, stroking the *boppli's* hand. "Is Jaden here too? Are you staying for supper?"

"*Jah*, we are," Martha said.

"*Gut*. I wanted to spend some time with these *bopplin* later." Emily kissed her niece on the cheek. "Too bad they're too small to take an interest in the kittens."

"How are they doing?"

"*Gut*. Titus has some bottles that he's going to bring over for them tomorrow."

"Ah." Martha shook her head. "Poor Titus. I really hope he finds a *gut* woman."

Emily felt her face flushing. "*Jah*. He seems like a *gut* man."

"Just so long as it isn't *my* woman, I'm *gut*." Jaden walked in on their conversation, her nephew in his arms.

Emily smiled and stared at Martha. "What does *that* mean?"

"*Ach*, Titus wanted to court me about the same time Jaden moved here," Martha explained.

"But he quickly found out she was already taken," Jaden chimed in, pecking her sister on the cheek.

"Really?" Emily's eyes widened. "I never knew that."

Martha sighed. "*Jah*. I really do wish him well. He needs someone special."

"I like Emily!" With his shirtsleeve, Ty wiped the strawberry juice off his face. "And her strawberries."

Indeed. Titus sighed.

"I can't wait for her to come over tomorrow!" Rose hadn't stopped smiling since Emily said she'd teach her how to make strawberry shortcake.

Me neither.

Ach, he needed to figure out something for tomorrow. *Jah*, he'd be bringing the kittens' bottles. But he wanted to do something a little extra, for her. Helen had always appreciated his gifts. She'd kept every one. Even made some of the petals from a flower bouquet into a bookmark she'd kept in her Bible.

He thought now about the conversation he and

the *kinner* had with Emily. Surely there was something... *that's it!* He knew exactly what he'd take her tomorrow. But to make it a reality, he'd better get to work.

As soon as the *kinner* retired for the evening, he'd slip outside to his shop.

FIVE

*E*mily stepped into Miller's Country Store and Bakery just as she noticed Sammy Eicher pulling in with an *Englisch* driver.

Her best friend Bailey's face lit up the moment she walked through the door. "Emily!" She promptly rounded the corner of the sales counter and smothered her in a hug.

Emily giggled. "It's *gut* to see you too. It smells *wunderbaar* in here. Well, I guess it always smells *wunderbaar* in here." She laughed again.

"That's probably the number one thing our customers say," her sister-in-law, Kayla, chimed in. "How are you doing, Emily?"

"*Gut*. How are you and Silas and the *kinner*?"

"We're well. Silas and Paul have a big order right now, so they've been quite busy. Shiloh's been pretty much running the household keeping her siblings in line."

"Judah got a car," Bailey whispered to Emily.

Kayla shook her head and frowned at her oldest *dochder*. "We're not talking about that, Bailey."

"And *Mamm's* expecting again," Bailey added.

"*Ach*, really?" Emily smiled. "Congratulations. I bet Silas is excited."

"*Jah*, and *Mamm's* been sick." Bailey frowned.

Emily mentally counted Silas and Kayla's *kinner. Bailey, Judah, Shiloh, Sierra, Daniel, Lydia, Lucas, Aaron, Emma, Caleb, and now this boppli.* "So, number eleven."

Kayla laughed. "Right. Wow, I never dreamed I'd have eleven children."

"I can imagine. Most *Englischers* have, what? Two or three?" Emily asked.

"I think that's about accurate," Kayla said.

Emily turned to Bailey. "No *boppli* today?"

"*Nee*, she's with Timothy. He's such a *gut dat*." Bailey grinned.

Emily's mind immediately flew to another *gut dat*.

Sammy Eicher stepped into the store. "Hello, ladies!" The kind older man had always been a chipper fellow.

"Hi, Sammy." Kayla smiled. "Here for potpies?"

"*Jah*, but I have a different request. Would Silas or Paul be willing to deliver a couple for me this evening?"

"Locally? Or where?" Kayla asked.

"*Jah*, here in Bontrager's district. Do you know Titus Troyer?"

Emily's head popped up and her ears snapped to attention. She glanced at Bailey, who stared at her curiously.

"*Jah*, they know Titus," Kayla said.

"If you could maybe have one of them stop by his place, leave the pies, and invite him to our men's group, I would appreciate it," Sammy said. "I invited him, but I think he'd be more receptive if one of the younger men extended an invitation too."

"I can ask Silas. I'm sure he won't mind."

"I'd appreciate that. And add something sweet for those *kinner* of his."

"I'll put in a few fry pies. Half price." Kayla winked.

"Perfect." Sammy grinned and handed over twenty-five dollars. "Keep the change."

"Nothing for your family today, Sammy?"

"Nah, I have a few potpies in the freezer yet. Miriam says I better not bring any more home or we'll be eating potpies for breakfast, lunch, and supper." He chuckled. "Which, I probably wouldn't mind but there'd be complaints from the *kinner*."

"Could you use some bread? I need to clear out

some of these shelves to make room for the fresh loaves tomorrow," Kayla offered.

"I suppose I can take a couple." He scratched his beard.

"Get what you'd like. No charge."

"*Denki*. Might as well send a couple of those over to Titus as well. I noticed he had some bread in his cart at Walmart." Sammy frowned. "He needs to find himself a *gut fraa*, I'm thinking. He's young enough yet."

Emily thought about her oldest brother, Silas, who'd been a widower before he met and married Kayla. They'd made a *gut* match, even though she and Bailey had been *Englischers* when they first arrived. Emily hardly remembered her *bruder's* first *fraa*, Sadie Ann, since Emily had only been about four when her sister-in-law and their unborn *boppli* passed away in early childbirth. She did remember the sadness in her *bruder's* eyes though. It was something she'd never forget.

No doubt, Titus had experienced that gut-wrenching sadness as well.

They exchanged goodbyes with Sammy as he walked out the door, and Kayla left to fetch Silas.

Bailey immediately spun around and faced Emily. "What was *that* all about?"

"What?" Emily smiled. That *was* what she'd come to talk to her friend about, but she didn't want to spill all her thoughts.

"Un-uh. Don't *what* me. I saw the way your eyes lit up at the mention of Titus Troyer's name."

"Well, what do you think of him?"

"I guess I never really thought much about him." Bailey shrugged. "More importantly, what do *you* think of him?"

Emily bit her nail. "He and the *kinner* stopped by my stand today."

"And?"

"I showed them the kittens. The little ones loved them."

"And?"

"Titus said he has some extra bottles that I could have. He's going to drop them by tomorrow."

Bailey's eyebrows lifted. "Okay?"

"He bought some tomatoes and strawberries and I mentioned strawberry shortcake, which he said he doesn't know how to make, so I offered to come over and teach his *dochder* Rose how to make it. And I think I might like him." The words spilled out of her mouth all at once.

Bailey giggled. "I think you do."

"You don't think...am I too young for him?"

"How old is he?"

"Ten years older. He went to school with Paul and Martha." She worried her lip.

"Well, that is quite a difference." Bailey shrugged. "How does he feel about it?"

"I don't know. I don't even know if he's interested in me."

"Did he smile a lot when he was there?"

Emily nodded.

"He likes you," Bailey said matter-of-factly.

"A lot of people smile. That doesn't mean anything."

"Did he meet your eyes when he smiled?"

"Well, *jah*, but—"

"He likes you." Bailey insisted. "Trust me."

"I hope so. I just...do you think it will be awkward? I mean, since he already had a *fraa* and all."

"Maybe a little bit. How did the *kinner* act around you?"

Emily smiled. "I think they like me."

"Well, that's what matters. If they like you, then he will like you. But it sounds like he already does."

"What do you think? Of the two of us."

"It doesn't matter what I think. But if you want to know, I just want you to find someone who will make you as happy as Timothy makes me."

Emily nodded.

"If you're thinking that people will talk, of course, they will. But who cares? You and Titus do what *Der Herr* is leading you to do, and don't worry about what anyone else thinks. If it's His will, He will make it work out." Bailey smiled. "Just look at me and Timothy."

"You're happy? Truly?"

"Well, our marriage isn't perfect. No relationship is. But that's okay. We love each other. And yes, for the most part we are happy. I'd marry Timothy again in a heartbeat, and I'm sure he feels the same way."

"I think maybe Titus and I would be *gut* together. We'd make a *gut* team, probably." Emily shrugged. "I don't know. It just seemed like we had a connection."

"Well. Then why don't you see where it leads? If you're going over to his place, it will give you a chance to get to know him and the *kinner* better. If you two get along well, then maybe you will become friends. If you don't, there's no law that says you have to continue a relationship with him."

"Right. Okay." Emily took a deep breath. "I guess I'm a little nervous. You know, since he's older and all."

"Don't be. If he's interested in you, he won't care about that."

SIX

Titus had just finished putting the dusting rag away when a knock sounded at the door. He frowned. Who could be visiting him and the *kinner* at this hour? Not that it was terribly late, but the sun was descending quickly.

He opened the door. "Silas Miller?"

"Hey, Titus. I hope I didn't catch you at a bad time."

"*Nee*, it's fine. Come in." Titus noticed a box in one of Silas's arms.

"Sammy Eicher stopped by the store and asked if I'd drop this off for you."

"What is it?"

Silas glanced down into the box. "Looks like a couple of Kayla's potpies, bread, and some fry pies."

Titus smiled and took the box from Silas. "That was thoughtful of him. *Denki* for delivering it."

"Kayla said Sammy talked to you today?"

"*Jah*. I met him at Walmart. Seemed like a friendly guy."

"*Ach*, Sammy's the best," Silas said.

"Would you like something to drink? Coffee? Or let me see what Rose has in the fridge." He walked over and opened the refrigerator door. "Looks like iced tea."

"I'd love some tea."

Titus poured both of them a glass, then handed one to Silas. He sat down at the table opposite of his guest.

"It's quiet in here," Silas remarked.

"*Jah*. The *kinner* are supposed to be straightening up their rooms. We're expecting company tomorrow." He wouldn't tell Silas it was his youngest *schweschder* that would be visiting. That would just be awkward.

"I see." Silas nodded. "Sammy wanted me to invite you to our men's fellowship. It's basically me, my brothers Paul and Nathaniel, my friend Michael— he's Sammy's *gross sohn*, my friend Josiah and you know Jaden, right?"

"Uh, *jah*. Kind of." He scratched the back of his neck. He still felt awkward around Martha's husband.

"Oh, yeah. And Timothy, too. It's a really relaxed

time. We usually have breakfast and study the Bible some. But mostly, we just talk about what's going on in our lives and encourage one another. You really should come."

Titus pondered the idea. It would definitely be a few steps out of his comfort zone. At the same time, it sounded like something he might need. He already knew most of the men, so maybe it wouldn't be too intimidating.

Titus rubbed the condensation on his glass. "Silas, may I...ask you something?"

"Sure. Shoot."

"Well..." He paused, gathering his courage. "You lost your first *fraa* too, right?"

Silas nodded. "Sadie Ann and our *boppli*."

"Oh, I hadn't realized..." Titus frowned.

"*Jah*, the cape dress hid it well. Not many knew."

"How did you get past that? How did you open your heart again to another woman?"

"With mine and Kayla's situation, it was a little different than normal. We both had thought Bailey's father was dead. I saw that they were alone in the world, and I felt *Der Herr* leading me to be a father to the fatherless and to care for a widow. Which, Kayla wasn't married to Bailey's father, but it seemed close to the same thing in my mind.

"And then, as we spent time together, we fell in love with each other. While it was true that they needed me, I think I needed them in my life just as much." Silas smiled.

Jah, Titus's situation was different than Silas's. "Also, I guess I'm kind of afraid that if I remarry, I'll always be comparing my new *fraa* to Helen. I don't want to do that."

"You *will* mentally compare them, there's no doubt about that. I guess it comes naturally. The thing is to not verbalize it. You don't want to cause discord between you and your spouse, so just don't go there. Appreciate each of them for who *they* are, who *Gott* made *them* to be as individuals."

"That's *gut* advice."

"You have your eye on someone?" Silas's brow lifted.

"*Ach*, maybe."

"I'd say go for it. I became a new man when Kayla and I married. Actually, I think I changed *before* we got married, now that I think about it. Love can make you do crazy things."

"*Jah*." Titus smiled. Like what he had planned to do tonight.

Was that love?

"Anyhow, regarding the men's fellowship, if you'd

like to come along, we meet Saturday mornings. Paul, Nathaniel, Timothy, and I always hire a driver to take us to Sammy's. Our driver has a van, so there's plenty of room for you to join us."

Titus took a sip of his tea. "I'm not sure. With the *kinner* and all..." he shook his head. "I already feel like they're with my *mamm* too much. You know what I mean?"

"I do." Silas nodded. "Let me handle that. I'm sure I can find someone to watch them for you. My *dochder* Shiloh is fifteen and she loves *kinner*. She'd be perfect."

Uh... "If you're sure."

"We'll swing by to pick you up around seven thirty. And don't worry about breakfast for yourself or the *kinner*. We'll have that covered." Silas smiled.

"Alright, then."

"I better get going." Silas stood from the table.

"*Denki*. For everything." Titus truly meant it. It was nice to know there were people around him who cared. It reminded him of the verse, *Look not every man on his own things, but every man also on the things of others.*

"You're welcome. And you can thank Sammy in person on Saturday." Silas appeared to be reading him. He reached over and clasped his shoulder. "You'll be glad you went."

SEVEN

$\mathcal{E}$mily's hands trembled as she pinned her apron in place. *Why am I nervous?* She picked up her mirror and examined her hair and *kapp*. It looked fine for now. But who knew what she would look like when Titus Troyer showed up?

"What's taking you so long, Emily?" her sister Susan hollered from downstairs.

She nibbled on her fingernail. She still hadn't mentioned anything to her folks or siblings about going to Titus's place this evening.

When she'd agreed to it, it hadn't seemed like a big deal. But now? *Ach*, just the thought made her stomach churn. Surely her family would misconstrue this as a date. Which it wasn't.

"Be down in a minute," she squeaked out.

She took a deep breath, then hurried down the stairs to help with breakfast.

Susan cracked eggs into a bowl, while *Mamm* fried up scrapple.

"I'll set the table," Emily said. She glanced over her shoulder as she removed the plates from the cabinet. "Uh, Susan? Do you think you can handle the kittens' feeding tonight?"

Susan turned and stared at her. *Ach*, she must suspect something. "Why?"

"I'm not going to be home. I have plans."

"What plans? Since when?" Susan's hand planted on her hip and she stopped her whisking.

"Since yesterday." She wouldn't say any more unless she had to. Too bad she hadn't prearranged something brief with Bailey as her way out of the house, so no one would suspect anything. But it was too late for that.

"I already planned to take the buggy," Susan said. Which meant she wouldn't be home to care for the kittens.

"I don't need the buggy," Emily said.

"You hired a driver?"

"*Nee*, I didn't hire a driver."

"Well, then—"

"Susan, *nee*," *Mamm* said. "What Emily is doing is none of your business." A smile played on *Mamm's* lips. *Ach*, did *Mamm* know?

"*What's* none of my business?" Now Susan stared directly at Emily. Her lips curved up in an impish smile. "You have a date with someone, don't you?"

Emily grunted. "*Nee*, it's not a date. I'm just going over to Titus Troyer's—"

"Wait. Titus Troyer? The widower?" Susan's mouth hung open. "You're kidding, right?"

What did she mean by that?

"What's wrong with Titus?" *Great*, now she sounded defensive.

"Well, for one, he's like old enough to be your *dat*."

Emily gasped. "He is not! He's only ten years older."

"Which means you were *four years old* when he finished school!"

"Susan..." *Mamm* warned.

"*Mamm*, tell Emily that Titus is too old for her," Susan insisted.

"Ten years isn't too old, *dochder*," *Mamm* said.

"It doesn't matter, because we aren't dating. As I was saying, before I was so rudely interrupted,"— Emily glared at Susan—"is that I'm going to the Troyers' to teach Rose how to make strawberry shortcake from my strawberries. That's all." Emily felt like pulling her hair out. Of course, she wouldn't. She'd spent way too much time making sure it was perfect for...

Her cheeks heated. *Ach*, she did like Titus.

"Well, if it's not a date, then I think it's mighty inappropriate." Susan offered her two cents. Again.

"How is that?" Why was she even encouraging this conversation? She should just stop talking.

"It's a *mamm's* job to teach a *maedel* those things."

"Well, in case you've forgotten, his *kinner* no longer have a *mamm*."

"That's my point."

Emily groaned just as Nathaniel and *Dat* walked in.

"What's going on in here?" Nathaniel's gaze slid toward *Mamm*.

"Your sisters are squabbling."

"Emily's dating Titus Troyer," Susan quipped.

"*Nee*, I am not!" Emily couldn't help the tears that formed at her outburst. She ran upstairs to her room. She refused to be badgered about Titus Troyer any longer. It wasn't anybody's business whether they were dating or not. Besides, he was a quiet, decent man. He didn't deserve to have people talking about him behind his back. What would he think if he'd heard that conversation?

Ach, she was such a *boppli*. Up here crying. But she attributed it to the fact that she was the baby of the family. Which meant she'd been teased a lot. She didn't mind it most times, but other times she felt it

46

went too far. Like with Susan.

She sighed. What would Titus think if he saw her up in her room sniveling like an adolescent *maedel*? Surely, he'd consider her too young and immature for a serious relationship. How did she think she even stood a chance with Titus Troyer in the first place?

With every turn of the buggy wheel closer to the Miller residence, Titus clenched the reins tighter. Why did this feel so much like a date?

A breeze kicked up, bringing the scent of his mountain fresh soap to his nostrils. *That* was why it felt like a date. He wasn't exactly in his *for gut* clothes, but he was clean and had a decent outfit on. If this were an actual date, he'd be wearing his Sunday best. And he wouldn't have the *kinner* with him.

"I can't wait to see the kitties again!" Ty bounced on the seat next to him.

"And I can't wait to take Emily to our house," Rose said. "Do you think she'll like my room, *Dat*?"

"I'm sure she will, Rose." And even if she didn't, he suspected she'd pretend she did for Rose's sake.

Having the *kinner* with him was a *wunderbaar* distraction and helped take some of the edge off his nervousness.

As soon as Titus spotted Emily's produce stand, he cringed. A young Amish man stood there, gesturing as though they were having the time of their lives. He *knew* she already had a suitor. He just knew it. A young woman as lovely as Emily wouldn't *not* have young men seeking after her.

"*Dat*, why are we going so slow?" Rose was too perceptive for her own *gut*.

Oh well, it was too late to turn back now. Besides, he still needed to deliver the kittens' bottles. If Emily decided not to come along with them, that was fine. Rose and the *buwe* would be disappointed, but they would get over it. Titus would just explain that sometimes other things come up. Like Emily's beau stopping by unexpectedly.

The *kinner* would be disappointed? Who was he kidding? *He* would be the one most discouraged out of the group, plain and simple. *Ach*, he shouldn't have gotten his hopes up.

Reluctantly, Titus pulled into the Millers' driveway. The young man who'd been at Emily's stand was no longer there. He must have taken off while Titus was lamenting his misfortune.

Emily met them at the hitching post, her smile reaching her eyes. "Isn't it a beautiful day?"

Titus smiled and nodded. "*Jah*. It's *wunderbaar*."

"Did you want to go right away or do the *kinner* want to see the *kittens* first?"

"You're still coming with us?" He couldn't get over his shock.

Emily's smile dimmed. "*Jah*. Well, I thought I was. Didn't you want me to teach Rose how to make the strawberry shortcake?" A puzzled look crossed her face.

"*Jah*, but I thought..." He pointed in the direction of her roadside stand. "Your boyfriend..."

Emily glanced toward the produce stand, her brow furrowed. Then all of a sudden, she burst out laughing.

He wasn't sure what was so funny, but he grinned in spite of himself. The *kinner*, too, saw Emily's amusement and began laughing as well.

"What are we laughing at?" Titus asked.

Emily attempted to speak, then erupted into a fit of laughter again. She blew out a few breaths, still giggling, then finally found her words. "That was my *bruder* Nathaniel."

"*Ach*, well, no wonder." He chuckled. "So, *no* boyfriend?"

She pulled her lips in, suppressing a smile, then shook her head. "*Nee*."

Titus felt like jumping into the air and shouting

"Hallelujah!" But, of course, he wouldn't and hadn't ever done anything like that.

"I...uh...brought the bottles," he said awkwardly.

"Great."

"And there's something else." He moved to the back of the buggy and lifted the flap.

Her eyes widened. "What's this?"

"It's a cage for the cats, so they won't be climbing out of the laundry basket."

Her mouth opened slightly. "Did you have this lying around the farm too?"

"*Nee*. I made it last night."

All of a sudden, she stopped and stared at him. "Titus." She inhaled a wispy breath. "You made this?"

He nodded. "Well, the pad inside used to be for the *bopplin's* changing table, but seeing as I don't need it anymore..." He shrugged.

"This is *wunderbaar*!" She ran her hand over the chicken wire and the latch, then opened the cage. "This is so thoughtful, Titus. *Denki*."

Ach, he hadn't expected her to heap this much praise on him. But he had to admit it felt *gut*. All he'd given her was a cage for the cats, but she made it seem like he'd given her fancy jewelry. If she was this happy about the kitty crate, what would she think when he gave her the other thing he'd made for her last night?

He pulled the cage out of the buggy. "You like it?"

"Very much."

Ach, he'd give her something every day if she'd smile at him the way she was now!

"Do you want it in the mudroom?"

"Yes, please. If you would." She led the way and he and the *kinner* followed.

Titus smiled to himself. *No boyfriend.*

EIGHT

*E*mily couldn't seem to wipe the smile off her face as she sat next to Titus in his buggy. Well, *almost* next to him. His youngest boy, Benuel, was perched between them. The two older *kinner* occupied the bench seat in back.

She could hardly believe men like Titus existed. Most males she knew didn't care much for cats; they only tolerated them. But seeing Titus with the kittens and knowing he'd crafted the kitty crate for her feline *bopplin* went beyond a kind gesture, to her thinking.

Thankfully, she'd be able to reward him with delicious strawberry shortcake tonight. She probably should have thought to bring something to make for supper as well, being it wasn't suppertime yet.

"I should have brought something to make for supper." She voiced her thoughts.

"*Nee*, we're fine. Your *bruder* Silas dropped by

with two potpies yesternight."

Ah, yes. She'd forgotten about Sammy Eicher's request. "I love Kayla's potpies. Have you tried one before?"

He nodded, turning on the crossroad that headed to the road that the school was on. "I believe I did have a little when Silas and Kayla hosted church in their home."

"That's right." She glanced back to make sure her bag of ingredients was still there, or that she hadn't forgotten it. It would be a shame to arrive at Titus's place without all the necessary ingredients for their dessert.

"When we get to the house, I'll put the potpies in the oven. After that, I'll need to tend to the chickens. The *buwe* usually help me with that. Rose can show you around the house while we're out chorin'."

"Okay." She clasped her hands in her lap. "How many chickens do you have?"

He was quiet a moment. "About a hundred. They're layers."

"Do you sell the eggs?"

"When we have too much stock, then yes."

"A hundred is a lot for just your family."

"It is enough." His hands tightened on the reins.

"I'm guessing you eat a lot of eggs, then?"

He pulled into his driveway. "*Jah*."

"I like eggs."

He glanced at her, then frowned. An unreadable expression crossed his face first, then one that seemed laden with pain. What was he thinking?

A few moments later, the five of them entered his house. It seemed bright and cheerful with the robin's egg blue curtains pulled back and the sun's rays filtering in through the windows. The house was smaller than Emily's family home, with only a single story.

Emily set her bag of ingredients on the dining table, where a lone lantern sat in the middle. The children seemed to disburse, leaving the two of them alone near the kitchen.

Titus kneeled by the woodstove, adding a couple of logs and some smaller dry pieces to fuel the fire. The house was quite warm, to Emily's thinking, but it didn't look like the Troyer property included a summer kitchen like her family home did. Summer kitchens were quite convenient in the warmer months when using a woodstove for cooking. They didn't have to worry about the house feeling like an inferno.

Rose joined them, her smile bright.

"Rose, will you open up some windows to let in the fresh breeze?" Titus glanced at Emily, a teasing smile on his lips. "We don't want our guest to overheat."

He moved to the refrigerator, then took the cold potpies and placed them in the oven. "They should be ready by the time the boys and I come back in." He called to Ty and Benuel, "*Kumm, bu*, let's go take care of the chickens."

Titus glanced back at Emily, pleasure radiating from his face. "Make yourself at home. Rose will show you around."

Emily stared after him when the screen door squeaked closed behind him and the boys. Every step he took away from her left her feeling empty somehow.

"*Kumm* see my room, Emily." Rose beamed.

Emily had a hunch this young girl missed having a mother. She followed Rose down a hallway.

"I'll show you the boys' room first. It's kind of boring." Rose opened the door to the last bedroom. Two twin beds covered in matching blue chenille bedspreads lined the walls, along with a dresser on each side. Each boy had a pegged wooden rack on the wall with their names inscribed. Rose noticed her looking at them. "*Dat* made those for the *bu*. He likes to do special stuff for us."

"*Ach*." Rose bent down to pick up a toy semi-truck and small die-cast tractor. "They're supposed to have

56

this cleaned up." Her exasperated tone made her sound like she was the boys' mother.

"It doesn't have to be spotless for me." Emily didn't want Rose to feel bad on her account. But it made her curious. "Does your *dat* like the house to be really clean all the time?"

"*Nee*, not really. But because you were coming to visit, he wanted us to clean up real *gut*."

"I see." The thought that Titus had been thinking of her being in his home warmed her from the inside out.

Rose moved to the door across the hall. "This room just has *Mamm's* stuff in it." She opened the door to reveal what appeared to be a craft room. A large armoire stood on one wall, with a treadle sewing machine opposite it. The door inside the room, that she guessed belonged to a closet, was closed.

"Do you know how to sew?" Emily asked. It was something every Amish girl was taught at a young age by her mother or, in Emily's case, her older sisters.

"My *mammi* is trying to teach me, but I'm not very *gut* at it yet."

"You'll learn. I didn't sew my first dress until I was twelve." Of course, she hadn't needed to. Being the youngest, she received her sisters' hand-me-downs. It was a rare occasion that she'd get a brand-new dress or apron.

"I wish I knew how." A wistful look glinted in her eye. "Do you think you could teach me, Emily?"

"Sure. I'd love to. That is, if your father doesn't mind. Maybe another day, though. We have strawberry shortcake to make tonight." Emily winked.

"Oh, *Dat* won't mind for sure. I think he likes you a lot. We all do."

Ach. "I like you all too."

"Emily, do you think you and *Dat* will get hitched?"

Oh, dear. This girl must be really longing for a mother. The thought crushed Emily's heart. It must not be easy being the only female in a household of males. "Well, I don't know, Rose. I can't really say. Your *dat* and I don't know each other all that well just yet. We'll have to see what *Der Herr* has planned."

"Well, then, I'll be sure to pray for it. *Dat* says we can talk to *Gott* about anything."

Emily smiled. "That's right."

Rose opened the door to the next room, which Emily guessed was adjacent to a bathroom, judging by the smaller door.

"This is my room." Rose's entire face lit up. "My special color is pink."

"I see. Wow." Nearly everything in the room

boasted the color, minus Rose's furniture, which was crafted of wood.

"*Mamm* made the quilt for me." She fingered the delicate rose pattern on the quilt.

"It's very pretty. She must've loved you a lot."

"It was in *Mamm's* hope chest, but *Dat* let me take it out after *Mamm* died."

Emily nodded, too choked up to trust herself to speak.

"*Dat* gave me some of *Mamm's* things." She held up a beautiful pink glass bowl. "*Dat* bought me the pillows too. They're fancy, ain't so?"

"They are. It sounds like your *dat* spoils you." Emily winked.

"He does. He made me this too." Rose touched a plaque on the wall with her name inscribed on it, similar to the boys', but this had a poem about daughters, encased in plexiglass. Around the poem were pink watercolor roses.

"It's beautiful. Does your *dat* like to work with wood?"

Rose nodded.

Emily hated to interrupt their special moment, but she thought she'd heard movement outside. "Should we set the table now?"

"I didn't show you *Dat's* room."

"I can see it another time, *jah*?"

"Okay."

"You'll have to show me where everything is." Emily followed Rose into the kitchen, and the two of them began putting out a place setting for each person. "Should we take out the drinks already or do we need to make something?

"I think we still have some tea."

"Perfect. Do you usually make sun tea?"

"Sometimes. But *Dat* likes the mix with tea and lemonade and it makes up real quick."

"Really? Will you show me what it looks like?"

Rose nodded and pulled out a yellow cylindrical container from the pantry. She opened the lid to show Emily. "It's pretty *gut* and you don't have to add sugar to it. Just water."

"May I try some?"

Rose scooped a little out into a glass, then filled it with cold water and handed it to Emily.

Emily sipped the tea. "Not too bad."

"I like fresh tea better, but this is *gut* in a pinch."

"I agree. Let's go ahead and mix some up, so there's plenty for your *dat*."

Rose pulled a half-full pitcher out of the fridge, then added more of the mix and water to it. "We have ice cubes too."

The screen door creaked open and the boys tromped inside carrying several egg cartons. Titus followed in behind them. The moment he lifted his eyes to hers, her heart did a little flip-flop. Again.

NINE

Titus entered the house to the delicious aroma of chicken potpie and a gorgeous smile that nearly buckled his knees. It was almost like a dream. Perhaps he'd entered the wrong home.

He surveyed the table.

"I think the potpies are ready. Rose and I brought out some chowchow, pickles, and cheese, if anybody wants some," Emily said.

"I want a pickle!" Ty grinned and plopped himself on the wooden bench at the dining room table.

"Not so fast, *sohn*." Titus looked at his overeager middle child. "Did you wash up first?"

Ty nodded. "Just did. In the mudroom."

"I can get out the potpies. Unless you'd rather?" Emily offered.

"I'll fetch them." When he picked up the hot pads, his hands were trembling slightly. *It's just supper with a beautiful woman. Jah,* like that would calm him. The last woman alone in his house that he hadn't been related to was Helen. No wonder why he was nervous!

Titus set the potpies on the table, then helped Benuel into his booster chair and took a seat. Everyone else followed his lead, except Ty, who'd already been patiently waiting. Rose sat immediately to his left and Emily sat next to her. He almost wished she'd sit next to him, but maybe that was inappropriate just yet.

Titus bowed his head for the silent prayer giving thanks to *Der Herr* for His goodness, for His provision, and for the company He provided on this *wunderbaar* night. When he lifted his head, the children passed him one of the potpies.

"*Nee,* let our guest take some first." The children weren't used to having guests over. *They* were usually guests at his *mamm's.*

"I can take some of this one," Emily pointed to the potpie in front of her.

Right.

Conversation, he reminded himself. It was something he'd never been that great at. He was happy to keep quiet and let others talk. He usually only spoke when something needed to be said. No need for small talk. Until now.

"Would you like some lemonade tea?" Emily offered.

"*Jah.*" He nodded. "*Denki.*"

Rose handed Titus's plastic tumbler to Emily and she deftly filled it, then proceeded to accept and fill everyone else's cup as well.

"Did Rose show you the house?" Titus set his fork down. No sense eating if he might be in conversation. Of course, if he was asking her questions, then she couldn't eat either. *Ach*, he wasn't really *gut* at this host thing. Helen had been great at it. He suspected Emily would be too.

"Most of it." She smiled. "I really liked the name plaque you made for Rose."

His face warmed. "*Denki.*" That was a *gut* sign. Hopefully, she'd like the gift he'd made for her as well.

"I didn't show her your room yet." Rose's smile broadened. "And guess what, *Dat*?"

Her smile was infectious.

"What?" Titus asked.

"Emily said she would teach me how to sew." Her voice brimmed with enthusiasm.

His gaze slid to Emily.

Emily held up her hands. "Only if it's okay with your *dat*."

"Of course, it is. Why wouldn't it be okay?" Titus

had nothing but admiration for this woman.

"I didn't know if maybe your *mamm* is teaching her... I mean...if she saw it as a bonding thing..." Emily shrugged. "I don't want to step on anybody's toes."

"I hadn't thought of that." He frowned. "No reason why she couldn't learn from both of you, ain't not?"

"If you don't mind." Her tone was hesitant. "And Rose doesn't."

"I don't mind at all." Rose beamed. *Ach*, it had been so long since his *dochder* had shown this much excitement about anything. Emily was truly *gut* for her.

"I wanna learn to grow strawberries like Emily," Ty's words came around a mouthful of potpie.

"It's a little late to plant them for harvest this year," Emily said. "But I'll have plenty. And if you want to come and help me pick strawberries, you can take some home for free."

Titus shook his head in wonder. *Ach*, she was so *gut* at connecting with the *kinner*.

"Can I, *Dat*? Can I?" Ty practically bounced off his seat.

"I don't see why not." Titus met Emily's eyes. Could she sense the amazement and gratefulness in his gaze?

She dipped her head.

Of course, this meant they'd be seeing each other even more. Did Emily enjoy spending time with them, as well? It seemed so.

After supper had been cleared, Emily set to removing the ingredients from her bag. Titus had taken the boys for their bath, leaving Rose and Emily in the kitchen to "do their thing," he'd said. She pulled out non-stick spray and her brownie pan and showed it to Rose. "Do you have one of these?"

"*Nee.*"

"Well, then, I'm glad I brought mine." Emily grinned. "It isn't totally necessary, but it makes things more uniform. You could just use a regular cookie sheet. Do you know what a cookie sheet is?"

Rose shook her head.

"Where are your baking things?"

Rose opened up a cabinet door and pointed inside.

Emily squatted next to Rose. "See those flat rectangular pans? Those are cookie sheets."

"Okay." Rose smiled. "Should I get them out?"

"*Nee.* We don't need them today." She tapped her chin. "Let me check the temperature on the stove. We might need to add more wood to it."

"I can get it," Titus said from behind them. "What temperature do you need it to be?"

"About four hundred would be *gut. Denki*." She then turned to Emily. "We'll need a large bowl and a spoon for mixing. I figured you would have those."

Rose found the things she'd asked for.

Emily handed the recipe over to Rose. "Now, I want you to make the dough. If you don't know what something means or you have any questions, I'll be right here to help. All of the ingredients are on the table, along with the measuring cups and spoons."

"What about the strawberries?"

"I cheated a little bit." Emily winked at Rose. "I made up the mixture last night because it tastes best if it marinades overnight in the refrigerator. It's very easy to make. You just wash and cut up the strawberries and mix them with the other ingredients in that top portion on the recipe."

"Marinades? What's that?"

"That's when the ingredients have time to mingle with each other. It makes the flavor stronger," Emily explained.

Rose stared at the recipe. "What is lemon zest?" Her lips twisted.

Emily figured Rose might have questions or want to make up the strawberry mixture herself, so she'd brought along the ingredients and gadgets just in case. She pulled out a lemon and her zest tool. "See those little holes." She pointed to her zest tool. "You just move it over the lemon peel like this."

Rose's smile widened. "May I try?"

"Sure." Emily handed both items to her charge.

"This is neat."

"My tool isn't very fancy, because I don't use it all that often. My sister-in-law Jenny has something called a Microplane that she uses at the bakery. It's quite handy. She uses it for all kinds of things, not just lemon rind."

"What kinds of things?"

"Oh." Emily shrugged. "To shave chocolate for the top of a cake or if she needs cinnamon fresh off the stick. Or finely shredded cheese. Those kinds of things."

"It sounds handy."

"It is. But my *mamm* doesn't like too many gadgets in the kitchen, or the drawers get cluttered." Emily pursed her lips.

"I think I might like to have one of those." Rose smiled. "Imagine chocolate or cinnamon in coffee soup!"

"*Ach*, that actually sounds really *gut*. Maybe we'll try it sometime." She pointed to the zester. "Gadgets are nice to have, but really, you can just use the small part of a regular old cheese grater if you're in a pinch. You don't really need all the fancy stuff."

Titus sat back, quietly observing Emily with his *dochder*. She was such a *gut* teacher, and Rose seemed to light up near her, or simply at the mention of her name. With every moment that passed, Titus became more and more convinced that Emily would make a fine mother.

But...what did she think of *him*? *Jah*, it was true their gazes had connected several times. But Titus got the impression that Emily Miller freely indulged others with her beautiful smile. That was who she was. He was nothing special. For all he knew, she simply considered him a nice older man. *Ach.*

The question, then, was *how* would he get her to notice him? What could he do to spark her interest? Or at least let her know that he was interested. How would she react? Would she be repelled?

He wasn't sure he possessed the courage to find out.

TEN

Emily instructed Rose to place her finished shortcake mixture in the oven. "It will take about twenty minutes. I'll remove the strawberries from the refrigerator, so they're not too cold."

Titus and the boys sat in the living room. The boys played with toys, while Titus quietly observed.

"And I'll make us some coffee," Titus offered. He stood from his hickory rocker and moved to the kettle on the stove.

Emily returned his warm gesture with a smile. "That sounds perfect."

The look of fondness in Titus's eyes made Emily think that he just might be a little bit attracted to her. Or that he at least admired her. Could that admiration possibly grow into something more?

"We should play a game." Rose's suggestion

distracted Emily's thoughts.

"That sounds like fun. What would you like to play?" Emily asked.

Ty jumped up, abandoning his toys on the floor. "Uno! Uno!" The boy spun around and disappeared from the room. Emily guessed it was to retrieve the Uno game. She loved the boy's enthusiasm but knew it likely translated to mischief. He kind of reminded her of her *bruder* Paul in his *rumspringa* years.

Little Benuel, on the other hand, was the opposite. As a matter of fact, he reminded her of Titus. Calm. Quiet. Even-keeled. Observant. But not without a personality of his own. She sensed there was more to Titus than met the eye. She already detected some of his teasing and playfulness. Benuel's personality remained to be seen.

Ty thrust the deck of Uno cards into Titus's hand. "Let's play?"

"How about we wait until after dessert, Ty?" Emily interjected. "It'll be ready real soon. You do like strawberry shortcake, ain't so?"

She turned to Rose. "Let's whip up the rest of that whipping cream, so it's ready when the cakes come out."

"Okay." Rose sat at the ready, whisk in hand. Emily had showed her how to make the whipped cream earlier.

"I'm going to check on the cakes," Emily said. "It smells like they might be ready."

She found a hot pad, and opened the stove door. "*Jah*, they look *gut*." She pulled out the pan and held it up. "Who's hungry?"

"Me! Me!" Ty ran to his place at the table.

Emily laughed and looked at Titus. "I think Ty's ready."

"So is his *dat*," Titus rubbed his belly. "*Kumm*, Benuel."

Emily and Rose quickly set small dessert plates and forks on the table. They dished out servings for each one, then took their seats.

Titus once again gave the blessing, then they all dug in. "*Ach*, this is *gut*!"

"I hoped you'd like it. It's a little different from the typical strawberry shortcake."

He nodded. "Not overly sweet."

"I like the way the sweetness mixes with a little bit of saltiness." She savored the flavors mingling in her mouth.

"I like your strawberries, Emily," Ty commented.

"Didn't your *schweschder* do a *gut* job making the strawberry shortcake? I think it turned out perfectly." Emily winked at Rose.

"It's very *gut*, Rose," Titus complimented. He

caught Emily's eye, his smile genuine. "*Denki* for helping her."

"It was my pleasure."

"*Ach.*" Titus stood up. "Almost forgot the coffee."

Ty vacated the table but returned when Titus did. He handed Titus something.

"*Denki*, Ty. But I don't think peppermints in my coffee will go that *gut* with strawberry shortcake."

"*Dat* likes peppermint patties in his coffee," Rose explained.

"With a little milk too," Titus added.

"I've never tried that before. But it does sound *gut*. Your *dat* is right, though. I don't think it would go too well with strawberry shortcake." Emily made a mental note to try the combination later. But it made her wonder. Did Titus enjoy other peppermint treats as well?

Titus brought two mugs to the table and filled them. "Would you like milk and sugar?"

"Sure, if you have it. Otherwise, black is fine. I like it either way. *Denki.*"

Ty's fork clattered on his plate. "All done. Can I have more?"

"I think one serving is enough," Titus said.

"It looks like you'll be able to have strawberry shortcake again tomorrow," Emily looked at Ty.

74

"*Gut. Gut.*" A tiny voice across the table said. A mixture of pink and white covered Benuel's lips and dabbed his nose.

"So he does speak," Emily said. "Well, I'm glad you like it, Benuel."

Titus chuckled. "It looks like you might need another bath, Benuel." He pinned Emily with a stare. "His speech kind of stopped when his *mamm*..."

Ach. She'd heard of things like that happening. "Do you think that's how he expresses his grief?"

Titus shrugged. "Couldn't say for sure. Seems so, maybe."

"Does he speak more when strangers aren't around?" She frowned.

"A little, but he's still not the same." The sadness in his eyes was back.

How she wished to help little Benuel. And his *dat*. Poor things.

"Let's play Uno now!" Ty said.

"We need to wash up these dishes first," Emily said. "Rose and I used quite a few."

"Dat washes the dishes when I make supper," Rose said.

"Well, then, I will help him," Emily insisted.

Titus cleared his throat, signaling he was ready to pray again. Everyone bowed their heads. When Titus finished, he instructed the kinner, "Ty, go clean yourself up. Rose, please help Benuel. Emily and I will clear the table and wash dishes. When we're done, we'll all play a round of Uno. Then we need to get Emily home."

The children did their father's bidding, while Titus and Emily cleared the table.

"You have great *kinner*," Emily remarked.

"I agree." He smiled as he smoothed a wet rag over the tabletop. "Really, though, I can wash up the dishes when we get back from dropping you off."

"I'd like to help, if you don't mind."

He nodded. "I appreciate it."

She rinsed several dishes in one sink to remove the stickiness, while Titus ran water in the other sink. Emily was happy their district allowed sinks instead of having to wash in bowls like some of the neighboring districts.

"*Denki* for coming tonight." Titus's voice was low.

"It was my pleasure. Thank you for supper."

"I'm afraid I can't take credit for that. It was Sammy Eicher and your *bruder's* doing."

"Still."

He washed a plate and set it in the rinse water in front of her. When she reached for it, his hand accidentally brushed hers, sending a wave of delight through her. *Ach.*

He cleared his throat. "Sorry." Had he felt it too?

"*Nee*. It's okay." She took a deep breath. "So, you enjoy woodworking and raising chickens?"

"I do."

"I saw what you did for the *kinner*. Are there more things in the house that you've made?"

He nodded. "*Jah*." He cocked his head to the side and she looked to where he'd motioned. A key rack that had "Titus and Helen" inscribed on it adorned the wall. Roses were etched on the wood next to each of their names.

"That's *wunderbaar*, Titus. Do you ever sell your things?"

"*Jah*. Sometimes at auctions and such. I sold some at the Christmas auction last year."

"I bet my *bruder* Silas would sell them in his store. They don't have anything like that."

His brow lowered. "Do you think they would sell?"

"I don't see why they wouldn't sell. They're nice. You could make a few different things just to see," she suggested. "You should talk to Silas. Or I could if you'd rather."

"*Nee*, I wouldn't want you to do that for me. I can talk to him."

"Okay."

"*Denki*, Emily."

She frowned. "For what?"

"For encouraging me."

She reached into the wash water and squeezed his hand without saying a word. No words were needed.

ELEVEN

*T*itus hated the fact that this evening would end soon. If Emily were a permanent member of their family, she wouldn't be leaving. Part of him was scared to death to ask her if she'd let him court her. The other part wished they could skip the courtship altogether and marry tomorrow. *Jah*, he knew the thought was absurd. He'd run her off for sure if he ever voiced it.

So he decided not to.

"Alright, *kinner*, it's time to get Emily home." He stood from the sofa. The Uno game had already been abandoned and they'd been enjoying casual conversation. Benuel slumped against the couch. He'd nodded off in the middle of the game.

"Aww, do we have to?"

"Yes, Ty. We can't keep Emily all night. She has to feed her kittens in the morning." *Although*...what would it be like to hold Emily in his arms? *Ach*, he hadn't considered holding any woman, save his *fraa*. Not even when he'd thought on courting Martha. Not since Helen. He shrugged off the inappropriate thought.

"But her *bruder* can feed the kittens tomorrow," Ty protested.

"*Nee*." Emily said. "My *bruder* works tomorrow. Your *vatter* is right. I need to get home. You don't want my *dat* to worry about me, do you?"

He answered with a sober shake of his head.

"Grab your hat and load up," Titus instructed.

The ride to Emily's home took a lot less time than he'd hoped. On a beautiful evening like tonight, when the weather was perfect, he could drive for hours with this *wunderbaar* woman by his side. The Indiana sunset had almost made its final descent, and remnants of light lingered on the horizon. Must be close to nine, by his thinking.

Benuel slept between the older two in the back seat, and Ty looked like he might be dozing off. Chances were, he didn't want to miss saying goodbye to Emily, and once he did, he'd be down for the count. Rose had kept quiet and he wondered what she was thinking. Was she hoping Emily would become a permanent part of their lives as well?

He glanced back and smiled at his *dochder*, before turning in to Emily's driveway. "We're here."

Ty perked up in the back seat, stood, and stuck his head between Titus and Emily. Benuel began crying, likely from being jarred awake by Ty, but Rose was quick to quiet him.

"Sit back down until we come to a stop," Titus reprimanded.

His son quickly obeyed.

Once at the hitching post, he instructed the children to say goodnight to Emily, then moved to tether the horse. Emily reached over and gave each of the *kinner* a hug before accepting his hand and descending the buggy.

The two of them strolled to the entrance of her home.

"*Denki*, again, for coming. The *kinner* had a *gut* time." He met her eyes. "And so did I."

She glanced toward the buggy, then her gaze moseyed back to his. "I did too. And not just because of the *kinner*."

He swallowed. *Ach*, this was the hard part. The vulnerable part. But she had said there was no beau. "Emily, would you—"

"Yes."

He chuckled. "You don't even know what I was going to say."

81

"I had an idea. But my answer is yes to whatever you're asking." Her smile was bright.

"That...could be dangerous." Especially since his mind was now going in a hundred different directions.

"I don't think you *can* be dangerous, Titus Troyer."

Ach. Well, then...

Without thinking things through, he stepped close, lowered his head, and brushed her lips with his. When she responded in kind, he tilted his head, kissing her more soundly. The heat of her hand on his chest seeped through his shirt, jolting his senses to life.

He needed to step away.

He broke contact, albeit reluctantly. His thumb grazed her lips, then her cheek. "You're wrong, Emily Miller." His voice sounded hoarse to him. "So wrong."

He couldn't help dropping his lips to hers once again. This time, he drew her into his arms, craving her nearness.

It wasn't until he heard the *kinner* rustling in the buggy, that he finally came to his senses. Then he remembered the gift he had yet to give Emily.

"*Ach*, that was nice," he whispered.

"*Jah.*" Emily's smile seemed shy, somehow.

"I have something for you. It's in the buggy. I'll be right back." Titus jogged to the carriage and uncovered the gift he'd kept hidden under a blanket.

He hid the gift behind his back until he came close, then presented it to Emily.

It was dark, but the moonlight shined down on them and provided enough illumination to see the gift.

Emily's hand moved over the smooth surface, then traced the letters he'd inscribed on the wooden plaque. "Emily's Garden Stand. I love it, Titus." She rewarded him with an all-too-brief kiss.

"I figured you could hang it out by the road."

"It's *wunderbaar*, truly. I think I'll do that." She reached for his hand and gave it an affectionate squeeze. "*Denki*, Titus. This was very thoughtful of you."

"*Da-a-a-t!*" Ty's voice called from the buggy.

Titus chuckled. "I never envisioned courting with *kinner* along. I guess I better get them home."

"Okay." She tugged in her bottom lip and he felt like kissing her again. But he probably shouldn't, otherwise Ty was liable to wake up the entire Miller household.

"*Guten nacht*, Emily." He grazed her cheek with a gentle kiss, then forced himself to trudge back to the buggy.

"Good night." Emily waved as they drove off.

Her smile and kisses would surely accompany his dreams as he slept this night. That was, if he could get any sleep.

With bated breath, Emily watched Titus's buggy disappear, then stepped into the house. She would have squealed and danced a jig if she were alone in her home. But doing so now would surely awaken the family. She was certain her heart might leap right out of her chest.

Her fingers moved over her lips reminiscing about Titus's *wunderbaar* kisses. *Ach*, she'd fairly swooned in his arms. Just like in the romance books she read. Now, she could relate. Was this how it felt to be in love? Her heart soared with everything good and pleasant and lovely. Nothing could make this night better.

She'd wondered if Titus could tell how inexperienced she was. She'd been kissed on the cheek before and had received a brief peck on the lips. But technically, tonight had been her first *real* kiss. And what a kiss it was! She had no idea *that* was how real kisses were supposed to be. It was fun and strange and exciting all at the same time.

Ach, she'd be fantasizing about it until she saw him

again. Of that, she was sure.

The way he'd made her feel, she wished she could kiss him all day long. Or for at least an hour. Did people ever kiss for a whole hour? Or would their lips get too tired? Maybe she'd ask Bailey about that. She would know, since she was married.

After tonight, she just knew that Titus was *the one*.

She smiled, thinking of the possibility of being a mother to three precious *kinner*. She already loved them, and she was pretty sure they were quite fond of her too. Well, Ty and Rose, anyhow. The verdict was still out on little Benuel.

When the evening had started, she'd been unsure of Titus's feelings and intentions toward her. But now? *Ach*, now she was certain sure their feelings were mutual.

Their future held promise. Lots of it.

TWELVE

During the course of their evening together, Titus and Emily had figured out a plan for the *kinner's* activities. After Rose had gone to school, he would drop off Ty to help Emily with strawberry picking and working the roadside stand. When Rose finished school, Titus would take Ty home with him and leave Rose with Emily for a few hours to sew, then he'd return for her.

It had been a *gut* plan, but Titus couldn't help but feel left out. He desired time with Emily too. Perhaps they could schedule a date and he could ask his *mamm* to watch the *kinner* for him. *Jah*, that was a *gut* plan.

As a matter of fact, as soon as he dropped Ty off and confirmed the day with Emily, he'd make a visit to his folks' home.

"I wish school was over already," Rose grumbled from the back seat of the buggy.

"I get to go help Emily right now," Ty boasted.

"It'll pass quickly, *dochder*," Titus attempted reassurance, but he knew how she felt. Although he'd be seeing Emily, he wouldn't get much time with her today, either.

He eyed Ty. "It's not nice to rub it in. You'll be starting school next year."

"I like school!" Ty's enthusiasm made him chuckle.

"You've never even been to school, so how do you know?" Rose challenged.

"They get to color pretty pictures for the wall," Ty said.

Titus chuckled at his *sohn's* simplistic ideas.

"You don't get to sit around and make pictures all day, *bensel*. It's hard work sometimes." Rose shook her head.

Titus was unsure what kind of hard work she would be referring to in the second grade, but he kept quiet. He enjoyed hearing the *kinner's* conversations.

"Well, I'll get to play outside too." Ty defended his theory.

"Not for very long," Rose answered.

Titus didn't want Ty to get discouraged, however. "I'm sure you'll get along just fine in school." He glanced back at the two *kinner*. "No need to squabble about it."

The children quieted down the rest of the way to the schoolyard. After Titus and the boys bid farewell to Rose, Ty could hardly contain his excitement. Titus shared the boy's enthusiasm, but internalized his feelings.

Ty practically squealed the moment Titus pulled in to Emily's driveway.

"How did your *date* with Titus Troyer go last night?" Susan's words were meant to rile Emily up, but instead she smiled.

"Susan," *Mamm* warned.

Emily appreciated *Mamm's* ready defense, but there was nothing Susan could say that would faze Emily this morning. Nothing would dim her joy.

"*Gut. Zehr Gut.*" Emily took a bite of her dippy eggs, savoring the flavors. It was interesting how everything seemed to taste and smell better this morning. As a matter of fact, the sun seemed to be shining brighter and the birds' songs louder. As if falling in love had unlocked her senses.

Susan gasped. "You mean, you're not going to correct me?"

"*Nee*," Emily simply said.

"*Ach*, so it was a date!"

"Maybe." Emily enjoyed keeping things from her nosy sisters, but she knew they'd eventually find out anyhow.

"Titus Troyer is courting you?" Susan snorted.

Just then, Emily heard the turn of buggy wheels outside. She quickly rinsed her plate and deposited it in the sink.

Susan snooped through the curtains. "He's here *now*?"

"Ty's helping me today," Emily said, as she donned her light shawl then slipped out the door.

Titus spoke with *Dat* at the barn while he tethered his horse. The moment *Dat* spotted Emily, he slipped back into the barn. When Titus turned around, Emily's heart got all fluttery again.

Titus's warm smile, the look of love in his eyes, and his simple "Hello" spoke volumes. How she wished they could steal away for another kiss. Goodness, had she already developed an addiction to his kisses? It seemed so.

"Would you like a cup of coffee?" she offered.

He scratched his beard, and a smile formed on his lips. "I'd love one, but I'd better not. I was a little late getting up this morning, so the chickens haven't been fed yet. I should get home."

Her enthusiasm deflated a little, until he leaned

close and whispered, "I laid awake thinking of you for too long last night."

Heat crept up her cheeks.

"Which reminds me," he continued, "I planned to ask my *mamm* to watch the *kinner* one of these days so we can spend some time together. Will Friday work for you?"

She couldn't suppress her smile. Titus wanted to go on a date? "*Jah*. Friday sounds *gut*."

Although, she usually prepared for the downtown Saturday farmers market on Fridays. Oh well, she'd just have to wake up extra early on Saturday or prepare Friday morning instead. Because her driver would show up at seven whether she was ready or not.

She thought about the farmers market. She'd never seen Titus and the *kinner* out there. It would probably be a *gut* place to sell his wooden crafts and the extra eggs his chickens produced. Maybe she'd suggest that on their date Friday. It would give them something to talk about.

"I'll see you this afternoon, then." He helped Ty out of the buggy.

"Can I see the kitties?" Ty's irrepressible expression made her think of the sun's rays bursting through the clouds.

"Of course." She took his hand. "Wave goodbye to

your daddy and Benuel."

Titus waved and winked as he set off down the driveway.

Ty tugged on her hand, not wanting to watch the buggy as it disappeared out of sight.

"You're just in time to help me feed them." Emily smiled down at her young partner.

"I like to feed kitties."

"*Gut*. Because they're mighty hungry right now."

"They didn't eat breakfast yet?" His eyes expanded.

"Nope, not yet." She pushed the mudroom door open to a chorus of meows.

"*Ach*, they're really hungry." Ty marched over to their crate.

"We need to get their bottles ready first. *Kumm*."

"I'll be back, baby kitties." Ty waved to the kittens as he followed Emily through the door to the dining area.

She led the way to the kitchen, which was empty now. *Mamm* and Susan must be tending to laundry. "First we need to get everything out. Their milk, the bottles, a funnel, and we'll need hot water from the stove."

"What's a funnel?" He laughed. "That sounds silly."

She pulled the funnel from her kitten basket and

handed it to him. "That's a funnel. I'll show you how it works. *Kumm*, let's sit at the table." She patted the bench.

Ty sat down next to her, his expression curious.

"Take the small part of the funnel and stick it into the bottle," she instructed and Ty did as told. "*Gut*. Now, I'll pour the goat milk in."

He watched intently.

"I only fill it halfway. Do you know why?"

He shook his head.

"Because the milk needs to be diluted. It's too strong for the little kittens' tummies. It's also too cold." She removed the kettle from the stove, then poured hot water into the other half of the bottle. She then twisted the cap closed.

Emily shook the bottle and squirted a little milk onto her wrist.

Ty laughed. "Why did you do that? Is your hand hungry?"

"No, silly." She tousled his hair. "That's to make sure the milk isn't too hot for the kitties."

"Oh."

She reached for his wrist and squeezed the bottle to drip some milk from the nipple.

"I don't even feel it." He stared at his wrist in amazement.

"That's how you can tell it's the right temperature. That it's not too hot. If it feels hot on your wrist, then it's too hot for the kittens. If it feels too cold on your wrist, then it's too cold for the kittens." She set the next bottle in front of him. "Do you want to pour the next one?"

His face lit up. "I can do it!"

"Okay, remember only to fill it half way."

He lifted the pitcher of goat milk. "I have strong muscles like *Dat*."

Emily smiled, recalling Titus's embrace the evening before. "Yes, you do. Do you need help?"

"Nope." He carefully poured milk into the funnel. "Uh oh. I think I put too much."

"That's okay." She removed the funnel and poured a little back into the pitcher. "There. Perfect. Now, I'll pour the hot water in because I don't want you to burn yourself."

She did as she said then handed the closed bottle to Ty. "Go ahead and check it."

He squeezed some onto his wrist and giggled. "It tickles."

"How is the temperature?" She put the pitcher of goat milk back into the fridge.

"It's *gut*."

"Okay, we better feed them now." Emily led the

way back out to the mudroom. "Go ahead and sit on the bench and I'll bring one to you."

Soberly, Ty followed her instructions, as though he had the most important job in the world. Which, in a way, it was. If they didn't provide nourishment for the orphaned kittens, the helpless creatures would die.

Emily took a rag towel from one of the pegs on the wall, picked out one of the calmer kittens, and began feeding the small creature. The first few seconds were the most hazardous, where sharp claws were concerned. "Fetch my garden gloves there in the corner and put them on. I don't want you to get scratched up."

Ty did as told, then sat back down.

She set the towel in Ty's lap, then handed him the kitten, bottle attached. "Now, put this hand under the kitty's arms, and hold the bottle with your other hand. Make sure the kitty stays on its belly when it's eating. If he stops drinking the bottle, he might not be done. Sometimes they need a break to burp."

"Like a real baby?"

"Yep, just like a real baby."

Within ten minutes, all four kittens had been fed. Since they were beginning to play more, Emily had gotten in the habit of leaving them out so they could explore. But today, she and her special helper had business to attend to. So, instead of leaving them out, she immediately returned them to their cage. They could get their playtime in after this evening's feeding.

"Are you ready to help me set up the produce stand now?" She asked as she rinsed out the kittens' bottles.

Ty nodded.

"Okay, this might require some muscles." She told the five-year-old. "We have boxes to carry out there. Do you think you can handle it?"

He nodded enthusiastically. "I can do anything!"

Emily chuckled. "Well, you sure are determined enough."

"What does 'determined' mean?"

"It means that you've set your mind to it. You told yourself that it's going to get done, so it will."

"Yep, I'm 'termined." Ty lifted the box Emily placed in his arms and followed her out to the roadside stand.

Emily's Garden Stand.

THIRTEEN

It was afternoon by the time Titus finished up his farm chores and pulled into his folks' country lane. Since he and the *kinner* usually visited on no-church Sundays, his arrival would be unexpected. The absence of Ty would also be a surprise.

He wasn't sure he was prepared to answer questions his folks might have—and they *would* have questions. Especially since he'd be asking them to watch the *kinner* on a Friday afternoon.

He braced himself as he pulled up to the hitching rail.

Mamm met him at the buggy, ready to greet the *kinner*. She received Benuel from his arms, then peered into the back of the buggy. "No Ty?" *Mamm* frowned.

"*Nee.*" Titus knew his pat answer wouldn't be sufficient, but he tried anyhow.

"Well?" She propped her free hand on her hip.

He finished tethering the horse. "Well, what?"

She shook her finger at him. "Don't you 'well, what?' me. You know exactly what I want to know."

He shrugged casually, as if his answer were of no consequence. "He's helping out on a farm."

"At five years old?" Her voice practically screeched.

"You and *Dat* started *me* early. Besides, it's just for today. He was interested in strawberries."

"Strawberries?"

"And kittens." Titus chuckled to himself.

"Who has strawberries and kittens?"

"The Millers." *Jah*, he was being vague, since they had several Miller families in their *g'may*.

"I see."

"Titus." *Dat's* cheery smile was contagious. "What brings you and the boys by today?"

"Not boys. Boy. He only has Benuel with him," *Mamm* informed *Dat*. "Ty's working on a farm."

"Oh?" *Dat* glanced at him.

"You got anything to drink, *Mamm*? I could use a drink." It was a shameless diversion tactic, but he *was* a little thirsty.

"*Kumm* to think of it, me too," *Dat* said. "I need a break, anyhow."

"Whatcha working on?" Titus asked.

"Bird feeder. Your *mamm's* been pestering me about building her one for some time now."

"I don't pester," *Mamm* spat the words over her shoulder, as she led the way into the house.

Titus and his father glanced at each other and guffawed. *Mamm* ignored them.

"I bet little Benuel's thirsty, too," *Mamm* said to his youngest. "Right, Benuel? Do you want *Mammi* to get you a drink?"

Benuel nodded once.

Titus and *Dat* took a seat at the table. Titus always enjoyed coming home. There was a sense of comfort and familiarity and belonging that accompanied his childhood home. Not to mention all the memories of him and his *schweschder* growing up in this house. Which made him wonder. "How's Laura doing?"

"She's *gut*. The *boppli's* about due here soon. Got a letter from her just yesterday." *Mamm* set a glass of tea down in front of each of them.

"Your *mamm* wants to go up there when she has her *boppli*." *Dat* grunted.

"Your father's not too thrilled with the idea," *Mamm* said.

"It would be different if they had a *dawdi haus* for us to stay in. Their house is already cramped as it is." *Dat* reasoned. "I like my space. And peace and quiet."

In many ways, Titus took after his *dat*. He appreciated peace and quiet as well.

"What brings you and Benuel by today?" *Dat* asked.

He eyed both of his parents. "I was hoping you'd watch the *kinner* for me on Friday evening. If you could keep them overnight, that would be great."

Mamm joined them at the table. "Overnight?" she stared at him. "Where are you going?"

"Home." His simple answer *should* suffice.

But not for *Mamm*. "Home? But I—"

Dat put his hand up. "Let the man have some secrets."

Mamm gasped. "Secrets?" Her mouth formed an O. "You don't have a date, do you?"

Titus pursed his lips together.

"Henry! Titus has a date." A smile spread across her face.

Dat eyed him. "You might as well spill it all now. Your mother will get nothing done until she knows every last detail."

Mamm jumped on it. "Who with? Don't tell me it's—"

"Let the boy speak, for crying out loud," *Dat* said.

He loved his folks. Truly. But sometimes...

"Emily Miller." He let out a breath. Just saying her

name sent his heart into a gallop.

Mamm's eyes rounded. "*Baby* Emily Miller?"

Titus chuckled. "I don't think they call her that anymore. Besides, she's twenty-four."

"Twenty-four? But you're—"

"Thirty-four. I know. I'm well aware of our age difference." Titus rubbed the condensation on his now-empty glass of tea. "Neither of us minds."

"So, you're already seeing her?" *Dat* had been right about *Mamm* wanting every last detail.

"In a manner of speaking, yes."

"*Ach.*" *Mamm* squeezed *Dat's* arm in excitement. "I have to go write Laura a letter."

Titus shook his head. "*Mamm*. You should at least wait until I'm out of the house before you start spreading gossip."

Mamm huffed. "Gossip? It's not gossip. Your *schweschder* will want to know. They've been praying for you, you know? We all have."

Tears now wet *Mamm's* eyelashes. She touched *Dat's* shoulder. "Henry, he's found someone."

"Now, *Mamm*. This is only our first real date. I don't want you setting your hopes too high. What if things don't work out?"

"Those *kinner* need a *mamm*," she insisted.

"I know they do."

"Wait. You said Ty is at *the Millers*?" Her voice went higher than usual. As though it had just dawned on her.

"*Jah*, he's with Emily." Titus smiled now.

She snapped her fingers. "Now it all makes sense."

"So, is that a yes to watching the *kinner*?" He lifted his eyebrows.

"Any time. Just bring them over."

"What about Laura?" Titus asked.

Mamm waved her arm in front of her face. "Laura's got people up there who can help. You need us more than she does."

Dat mouthed a "thank you" and Titus chuckled.

Jah, he loved his folks.

FOURTEEN

Poor little Ty had conked out before his *dat* arrived to pick him up. Emily enjoyed spending the day with the boy, but she had a feeling he missed his father. He'd asked about Titus a couple of times. She sensed that the *kinner* weren't separated from their father often. Ty had probably eaten as many strawberries as he'd picked, but she had still readied a basket for him to take home.

Seeing Titus again in the afternoon, when he'd picked up Ty and dropped off Rose, made her spirit soar. She couldn't help but feel like a horse with a carrot dangling in front of her, just teasing her, and out of reach, though. *Ach*, she longed to have him all to herself for a little while.

He'd informed her that he had cleared things with his folks regarding babysitting for their date on Friday. Friday. That meant she'd have to go a *whole* day, *nee*, almost *two* whole days, without seeing him.

Funny that a week ago she'd hardly known he existed. She'd known who he was, but had never even considered that he might be the one for her. They'd grown up with an entirely different set of peers. Him, with her brother and sister, and her, with Bailey and Timothy. A decade apart.

Rose's enthusiasm when she arrived at Emily's rivaled Ty's at the beginning of the day. She'd also helped Emily feed the kittens.

Now, the two of them occupied the *dawdi haus*. No one had lived there since her *bruder* Paul, and before him, their oldest brother, Silas. *Mamm* used the empty space to work on her quilts and their sewing projects.

"Did you remember to bring an extra dress?" Emily asked Rose.

"*Ach, nee.*" She covered her mouth, and worry dimmed her eyes.

"That's not a problem. You can change into one of my old dresses while we use your dress. Then you can put it back on. *Kumm.*" Emily led the way back into the main house and up the stairs to her room. Rose followed.

Rose gasped as she stepped into Emily's room. She glanced around at the treasures Emily had collected for her future home. "Your special color is blue?"

"It's actually a bluish-green color called aqua." Emily opened her hope chest and pulled out an old dress. "Here. It might not fit you perfectly, but it should be fine for a while."

"I like the color."

"It's pretty, *ain't not*? I wore that for my *bruder* Paul's wedding." Emily smiled. That seemed like a lifetime ago, yet she remembered it like yesterday. "It'll be a little big for you. I'll go out and let you try it on."

Emily stepped out of her room to give Rose privacy. "Let me know if you need help," she called through the door. Of course, if Rose had been without a mother for... Emily frowned. How long had it been? She wasn't even sure. But if she been without a *mamm*, chances were, she was accustomed to fastening her own dresses. Unless her *dat* helped her, which was a possibility.

She'd been saving that dress to give to her *dochder* someday—if she ever had a *dochder*. Perhaps that future *dochder* was trying on her dress right now. Emily smiled at the thought.

Several minutes later, the door creaked open and Rose stepped out. "It's kind of big."

Emily smiled. "*Jah*, but the color looks *gut* on you."

"Here's my dress." Rose handed the dress she been wearing to Emily.

"Okay. We can get started now." Emily led the way back to the *dawdi haus*.

She opened up a couple of drawers and pulled out a few bolts of material. "Go ahead and pick which color you'd like for your dress."

"I like this one best." Rose fingered a purple fabric.

"Okay. We're going to use your dress to make our pattern." Emily showed Rose how to make a pattern by using paper grocery sacks, then handed Rose a pin cushion shaped like tomato.

Emily unrolled the bolt over a large table. "Now pin your pattern onto the fabric, then I'll show you how to cut it."

Rose did as told, and carefully followed all the instructions Emily had given her. A few hours later, Rose's new dress was ready to try on.

Emily smiled as Rose modeled her dress. It wasn't perfect, but it was very *gut* for a first try.

"What do you think?" Rose spun around, happiness shining in her eyes.

"It looks *wunderbaar*," Emily encouraged. "Do you like it?"

Rose giggled. "Very much so! I can't wait to wear it to school."

Emily's mamm knocked on the door of the *dawdi haus*, then stuck her head in. "Emily, why don't you invite Rose and her family to stay for supper?"

Emily eyed Rose. "Would you like that?"

"I would love it. We all would." Rose's enthusiasm was contagious.

"*Gut*," Emily's *mamm* said, "Because I'm going to enlist you two to help me make it."

"Well, Rose, it looks like you better change back into your dress, then," Emily suggested.

"Okay."

Emily greeted Titus the moment he pulled up to the Millers' hitching post. "Would you like to stay for supper?"

He leaned close. "Anything that allows me to spend more time with you is a definite yes."

The hue in her cheeks pinkened a shade.

He hopped down and tethered the horse. He would have claimed a kiss if he knew no one was watching.

Emily helped the boys down. "Are you hungry?"

"*Jah*," Ty grinned. "Are we having more strawberries?"

"Not tonight. I think you ate enough of them

today, don't you?" Emily laughed.

Ty shook his head.

"His lips are still stained." Titus chuckled. He reached for Benuel's hand and followed Emily to the house.

The last time he'd darkened the door of the Miller home had been when he'd come to court Emily's oldest *schweschder* Martha. But this time was different. He hadn't come as an interloper this time; this time he'd been invited by a beautiful young woman whom he'd been falling in love with more every hour, it seemed.

He briefly wondered if there was some sort of rule that said you had to court for so long before making things permanent. *It's only been three days.* Three days since they'd "officially" met, although their families had known each other for quite some time and they'd both been born here in the community. His cousin Amy had been best friends with Emily's oldest sister since they were scholars. So it wasn't as if they were strangers.

He tried to think of other widowers and how long it had been before they remarried. His first *fraa* had been gone long enough, but that wasn't the issue here. Had Emily already been baptized? If not, that could be a hurdle. But, at twenty-four years of age, he highly doubted that she wasn't an official member of the *g'may*. And if she was, there was really nothing standing in the way. Widows and widowers didn't have to wait for the normal wedding season.

But what if Emily wanted a big wedding? Which, she very well might. Even so, they wouldn't have to wait as long. Would he scare her off if he talked of marriage already?

Love is patient. Jah, he'd heard those words before. But they were awfully difficult to live by.

It wasn't that he wanted her in a physically intimate way, although he did look forward to that part, but he wanted to be near her. He wanted her in his and his children's lives. In their home, living amongst them. He wanted to wake up to her breathtaking smile every morning and draw from it throughout the day. He wanted her presence.

"I hope you like beef stew," Emily's words pulled him from his fantastical musings.

"Dirt would taste *wunderbaar* if you were sitting by my side."

A sweet melodic laugh erupted from her lips. "Well, this will taste much better than dirt, I assure you. *Mamm's* beef stew is the best. Especially when you dip your bread into the juice."

He removed Benuel's hat and placed it inside his

own, then set them on the peg just inside the door.

"Titus." Nathaniel offered a handshake and a smile. "*Gut* to have you here."

"It's *gut* to be here." Titus nodded as they walked further into the house. Nathaniel was a bit younger than him, but they'd been in school together and had always gotten along well.

Rose burst into the dining area. "*Dat*, wait till you see the dress Emily helped me make!"

"You did the work, Rose. I just guided you." Emily met his eyes. "She did a *gut* job."

Titus shared a pleased smile with his *dochder*.

Emily's mamm popped her head into the dining area. "Nathaniel, is your dat inside? Will you let him know supper is ready?"

She didn't wait until Nathaniel responded, but disappeared into the kitchen again.

Emily's older *schweschder*—he couldn't remember her name—set bowls and plates on the table. She eyed him with curiosity, and he dipped his head to say hello. Her eyes widened, then she whipped around and disappeared into the kitchen like her mother had.

Okay, then.

Emily nodded toward the table, gesturing for him to sit down.

He leaned close and whispered, "I'd rather wait for

your *dat* to sit first." He didn't want to disrespect her father. Besides, he wanted to be told where to sit instead of assuming.

He sighed in relief when Emily's father finally entered the room. They all took their seats and Emily's father bowed his head to pray.

Titus uttered his own prayer.

FIFTEEN

"I think my folks like you," Emily said, as she and Titus walked along her family's pond after supper.

"Even though I beat your *dat* at checkers?" He lifted a brow.

"He probably let you win." She smiled.

He stopped walking and stared at her. "What?"

"He does it all the time, especially with the *kinskinner*. He's actually quite *gut*. So much so that no one wanted to play him anymore." She shrugged. "I think he figures that he'd rather have an opponent and let them win, than to not play at all. No one wants to lose all the time."

"But your *dat* does?"

"I think just knowing that he can win is enough."

"I see." He reached for her hand, intertwining their fingers. His gaze went to the water gently lapping at the edge of the pond. "This is nice."

"Is there a pond on your property?"

"*Nee*. Too dangerous for the *kinner*. Ty's too curious for his own *gut*." Titus shook his head. "I can't imagine losing another..." His words trailed off.

Emily's chin quivered. She'd always been overly sensitive to other people's pain. "I'm sorry. About your *fraa*."

"It was over two years ago. I should have moved past this." He shoved a tear away.

She lightly touched his forearm. "I don't know if a person can ever get past a loss of that magnitude. She was a big part of your life. Part of who you are—who your *kinner* are."

"You're right." He placed his hand over hers, then turned to face her. "But I need to move on. I want to move on. With you."

"What can I do to help you?" She reached up and touched his cheek, her eyes searching his.

"You're doing it." He dipped his head and met her lips with his, while a warm breeze danced around them.

His kisses tasted of coffee and peppermint, making her think of Christmastime and everything good and wonderful and right.

The unexpected surprise of being invited to stay for supper at the Miller home had been more than Titus had hoped for. Even now, two days later, he could taste the delicious beef stew Emily's *mamm* had made. And he'd probably relived his and Emily's special moments by the pond a thousand times. Especially the kisses.

Excitement surged in his gut as he prepared for their date tonight. He'd dropped the *kinner* off at his folks' place. He'd gone into town to fetch the items he needed to make tonight memorable. He'd donned his for *gut* clothes and a dab of cologne he hadn't worn in eons. Everything was set to create a perfect romantic evening.

When he approached Emily's driveway, his horse already knew to turn in. He'd been here nearly half a dozen times within the last week. It was beginning to feel quite familiar.

Emily's father lifted a hand in the air when he spotted Titus driving down the lane, mirth sparkling in his mien. Titus liked Emily's family, although being around her sisters felt a little awkward.

Emily stepped out of the house before he'd finished the journey, so he decided not to tether his horse. Instead, he made a U-turn and brought the rig to a halt. As he reached for Emily's hand and helped her up into the buggy, his senses nearly exploded. *Ach*, she looked and smelled like a dream. She sat on the bench seat beside him, her eyes revealing that she was just as thrilled about this evening as he was.

They waved to her *dat* as they exited the driveway, heading to their destination.

"Hi." He knew his grin must be stretching from one ear to the other, but he couldn't help it. Emily just did that to him.

"Hi." She smiled right back, albeit somewhat timidly.

"You look *wunderbaar*." His gaze slid over her attire.

"You smell *wunderbaar*," she returned.

"So do you." His eyebrow hitched.

His free hand inched toward Emily's, then his fingers grazed hers. He adored the smile playing on her beautiful lips. The ones he planned to taste this evening.

"What color do you call that dress?" He was pretty sure he knew, but he wanted her thoughts.

"It's aqua. Do you like it?"

"I think it's my favorite."

"Really?" Her smile broadened. "It's my special color."

He nodded. "Rose mentioned that to me."

"She did?"

"*Jah*. And she wore her new dress to school yesterday. Said all her friends loved it."

"That's *gut*." Emily wore a satisfied smile. "Hopefully, it gave her some confidence in her sewing abilities."

"I think so. She asked to use Helen's sewing machine. Said she wanted to make something special, but that she couldn't tell me what it was."

"She has a *gut* heart. Like her father."

He frowned. "Do you think so? That I have a *gut* heart?"

"From what I've seen, *jah*. You are admirable, Titus Troyer." Her fingers slid between his, and she gently squeezed his hand.

"Well, my thoughts aren't always pure, so don't lift me too high." He caught her staring at him.

"Tell me whose thoughts are. We all sin."

"For sure."

A breath of contentment escaped Emily's lips. "Where are we going?"

"You'll see soon enough." He turned onto the street that led home.

"To your place?"

He nodded, attempting to conceal his overwrought enthusiasm. He hoped she would think their evening was as special as he anticipated it to be.

When he stopped in front of the house, he helped her down and slipped her a note.

Curiosity danced in her eyes as she fidgeted with the note.

SIXTEEN

*E*mily's heart flip-flopped. What on earth did Titus have planned for their date?

"Read it," he encouraged.

She opened the slip of paper.

"Please have patience as I put the horse in the stable. You may find your next note inside on the table."

She giggled. "You want me to go inside?"

He nodded and kissed her cheek. "Wait for me there."

Emily watched forlornly as her handsome date walked off with the horse, then sighed. She looked down at the note, then followed the directions.

Inside, the house was a little dark, but a lantern flickered on the table. She walked to it, then turned up the wick. Near the lantern was another note like the one she'd just read. She opened the paper and read the words.

Having you in my life feels like a dream.

To find your next clue, walk down to the stream.

Titus walked in just then.

"The stream? I didn't know you had a stream." What other surprises did he have in store?

"Sure do. But first, we'll need this." He lifted a basket from the counter.

Her jaw dropped. "A picnic?"

His eyes twinkled as the light from the lantern reflected off of them. "Perhaps."

"Lead the way, because I have no clue where we're headed."

He chuckled.

"You're having fun with this, aren't you?"

"I hope you are too." He touched her shoulder and looked into her eyes. She saw a touch of worry in their depths.

"I am." She stepped on her tiptoes and kissed his cheek. "You're a sweetheart." She pulled his hand. "*Kumm*, show me the stream."

"*Jah*, okay." Basket hanging on his arm, Titus led the way. Once out of the house, he slipped his free hand into hers. "Tell me something about you that I don't know."

"Okay. Like what?"

"Something easy. What's your favorite color?"

"Aqua."

He chuckled. "Okay, I kind of suspected that. Your favorite food?"

"*Nee.* You have to tell me your favorites too."

"Okay. Blue." He shrugged.

Emily laughed. "There are a gazillion shades of blue. Which one?"

"I guess it's between true blue and dark blue. I wanna say it's called azure or admiral? Anyhow, I have a shirt at the house that color. I can show you later."

"Good enough. Okay, my favorite food is fruit."

"Fruit?"

"Well, it has to be ripe."

"What kind of fruit?"

"Any. I don't know if I've ever tasted fruit I don't like."

"Hmm. How about lemon?"

"I love lemons. I just can't eat a bunch of them at one time."

"What about those orangey-reddish-greenish fruits that come from Mexico?"

She laughed at his expression. "You mean mango? *Ach*, mangos are definitely at the top of my favorites list."

"I confess I've never had one."

"You've never tried mango?"

"I was kind of afraid of them."

Emily laughed again. "The trick is to pick the right one. With mangos, you don't want too firm or too squishy. If you press it with your thumb, it should yield just a little bit."

He chuckled. "I'll trust you on that one."

"That's it. Next time I go shopping, I'm buying you a mango."

He twisted his lips.

"Don't be a scaredy cat. They're delicious." She closed her eyes. "Mm...wish I had one now."

"Well." He grimaced. "I didn't bring any mangos, but I do have something you might like. I was going to save it for dessert, but..."

He stopped walking. "This is the perfect spot." He set the basket down and opened it, then removed a rectangular pillow-like thing. He unzipped it and it unfolded into a padded picnic blanket.

"That's neat."

"Found it at Big Lots."

"I like that store."

"Me too." He patted the blanket. "Have a seat."

She did as instructed.

"Okay, now close your eyes."

She stared at him. "Close my eyes?"

"Yes, just trust me. It'll be *gut*."

"Okay." She giggled.

"Now open your mouth."

"Titus."

"Just do it, please."

Reluctantly, she did as he asked. "I feel weird."

"You can't talk."

She smiled.

"You can't smile either." He laughed. "Your mouth isn't open."

She attempted to open her mouth and keep a straight face. She heard him rustling something.

"Now take a bite," Titus instructed.

She bit down into the yummiest dessert ever invented—chocolate covered strawberries! The delectable flavors exploded in her mouth. "*Ach*! This is delicious! May I open my eyes now?"

"Yes." A satisfied look displayed on his face.

She looked around her and discovered she was surrounded by a feast. Not only were there chocolate covered strawberries, but fried chicken, macaroni salad, coleslaw, green beans, and rolls. "*Ach*, Titus!"

"Do you like it?"

She leaned toward him and planted a bold kiss on his lips. "I love it!"

He groaned. "I love *that*. Come back here."

She indulged him with another kiss, delighting in

the sound of pleasure that escaped his throat.

"Emily." He pulled back, eyes wild with desire. "We can't do that."

She giggled. "I liked it too." Her heart still felt like it was beating a hundred miles an hour.

"*Jah*, but..." He sighed and rubbed his beard. "We should eat now."

She took the plate he offered and put a little of each thing on it.

"Uh-oh." He pulled a note from under the basket. "It didn't exactly go as I thought, but go ahead and read it anyhow."

She did.

"Later this evening I have planned a treat.
Open the basket now, so we two can eat."

"I know we're already eating but go ahead and open it."

She opened the basket, wondering what else he might come up with. "What's this?" She pulled out a wrapped box.

"A little something special for you." He grinned. "But don't open it until we're finished eating."

"Okay." She took a bite of her fried chicken. "This is *gut*."

"I can't take credit for any of it. I bought it all at the store."

"Still. Hey, you never told me what your favorite food was."

"Burgers."

"Hamburgers? Really?"

"Well, seasoned and grilled just right with a toasted bun and the perfect condiments."

"And do you know how to grill and season these burgers just right?"

"I do. How about I make some on our second date?"

"Second date or fourth? It kind of feels like this is our third date, doesn't it?"

"In a way. Although, we weren't alone the other two times. But if you want to count this as our third date, that's fine with me." He grinned.

"We weren't alone, but you still managed to sneak in some kisses. That means they were dates."

"Okay, you win. They were dates." He chuckled.

SEVENTEEN

S
o far, the night had been amazing. Not exactly how Titus had planned, but amazing nonetheless.

As soon as they cleaned up their dinner mess, he prompted Emily to read her next note.

He loved the cute faces she made when she read the notes. Sometimes, like now, she'd scrunch up her nose and he felt like planting a kiss on it.

"We met at your garden stand, but it wasn't by chance.

Please open your gift and allow me a dance."

She stared at him, confused. "A dance?"

He didn't say anything, but nudged the gift toward her.

She giggled as she opened it. "You're spoiling me, you know."

"I hope so." He couldn't stop smiling if he tried.

He was certain that he was enjoying this even more than she was.

Her eyes grew wide as she pulled her gift out of the box. "Titus! You didn't...did you make this?" She grazed her hand over her name inscribed on the top, then lifted the lid of the wooden jewelry box.

He nodded. "It plays music. The turner is on the bottom."

She held the jewelry box up and turned the wind-up key. When she let go, the sweet melody began. "*Ach*! *You Are My Sunshine*." Tears surfaced in her eyes. "I love this song."

He felt like saying, "I love you," but he suspected she already figured as much. "Let's go down to the stream and have our dance?"

They stood from the picnic blanket and he led the way to the stream. On the bank, he reached for her hand.

"I've never danced before," she confessed, as she set the music box down. She took his hand and allowed him to draw her near.

"Just put your arms around my neck," he instructed. He'd actually never danced either, but he'd seen people on television before. It didn't look too difficult.

He wrapped his hands around her waist and pulled

her close, then pretended he knew what he was doing by swaying back and forth. He was tempted to kiss her, since she was so close, but he refrained from doing so.

They kept dancing, even after the music stopped. Eventually, he gave in and kissed her on the mouth, resulting in unfulfilled desires. Likely for both of them.

They sat on a rock and enjoyed nature for a little while. The stream was like a lullaby that could calm a weary soul.

He pulled a note from his pocket and handed it to her.

She read the words he'd penned.

"Every cell in my body has now come alive.

Go back to the quilt to reveal note number five."

He shrugged. "I don't know if you can call the picnic blanket a quilt or not."

"It doesn't matter. I want to read number five." She clutched her jewelry box from the rock she'd set it on, and they continued toward their picnic site.

"It's the last one," he warned. *And hopefully the best.*

She arrived at the quilt and glanced around. "Where's the note?"

"You'll have to find it." He grinned.

"It's not in the picnic basket, is it?"

"*Nee.*"

"*Ach*, the pocket?"

He shrugged.

She opened the pocket on the blanket and pulled out a velvet pouch. "What is this?" She stared at him.

He nodded toward the pouch.

She opened the draw strings, then peered inside. Turning the pouch upside down, she allowed its contents to fall into her hand.

"Titus!" She breathed out his name, placing a hand over her heart. "Are you...? Is this...?" She fingered the two wedding rings.

In their district, one of the wedding customs was to hide two rings inside the bride and groom's cake. When it was served to the wedding party, one man and one woman would discover the ring in their slice of cake. Superstition said that they would be the next in line to get married, but not necessarily to each other.

He encouraged her to open the note.

I want to be near you for the rest of my life.
Will you do me the honor of becoming my wife?"

Tears shimmered in her eyes as she stared at him. "Titus, are you serious?"

"I'm dead serious. I love you more than I can stand it, Emily."

Her hands shook. "I...I don't know what to say. I mean, yes, but probably not too soon."

He nodded. *Yes was good, right?*

"When were you thinking?"

"I was going to leave that up to you. I'd marry you tomorrow, if I could."

"*Ach*, Titus." She shook her head. "I wasn't expecting this at all."

"I hope it's a *gut* surprise?" He couldn't help the vulnerability in his voice.

She covered his hand with hers. "A very *gut* surprise. Just unexpected." The curiosity in her eye was back. "Did you do all this for your first *fraa* too?"

"*Nee*." He chuckled. "I actually went to the library yesterday and checked out a book on creative dates."

"*Ach*, really?"

"*Jah*, really." He stood from the blanket and proffered his hand to help her up. "Let's go back to the house and enjoy some coffee now?"

"Coffee sounds perfect. Especially if you have any of those peppermint patties I can taste in your kisses."

He chuckled. "I might have one or two."

"Peppermints or kisses?"

"Both." He raised his eyebrows twice.

EIGHTEEN

Emily had stayed with Titus for as long as was appropriate, which meant she'd slipped into bed around two that morning. In spite of not having to wake up as early as usual, she was still tired. No doubt, she'd be tempted to doze off if the farmers market was slow today. But that wasn't likely to happen. Not during peak season. Certain folks in the surrounding communities relied on her for their fresh vegetables and fruit, especially the organic varieties.

She stretched and yawned and attempted to wipe the sleepiness from her eyes. She'd definitely be frequenting the downtown coffee shop today. She'd probably be their best customer. Which made her think about Titus's peppermint coffee kisses.

Titus. Her future husband.

In all her exhilaration, she could scream. But her family members likely wouldn't appreciate it.

Especially since Susan hadn't awakened yet. Where had *she* gone last night? Emily wondered.

"*Gut* to see you finally found your way home," *Dat* said as her feet hit the bottom step.

"Did you wait up for me?"

"Only for as long as my eyelids would allow. Conked out around midnight, I'd say." *Dat* sipped his coffee.

"I need to hurry. I'm running later than usual." She'd have to take her breakfast at the farmers market today.

Fortunately, set-up didn't begin until eight. The outdoor market ran from nine to twelve on Saturdays, from June till September.

"I'll help you gather your things, *dochder*," *Dat* offered. This was their Saturday morning ritual during the farmers market season.

Minus the cats. They were new to the equation. Which reminded her. "*Mamm*, could you see that the kittens get fed? I won't have time to do it."

"I'll have your *schweschder* tend to it once she gets up." *Mamm* replied.

Susan would be *thrilled* to hear the feeding duties had been dumped into her lap, but it couldn't be helped.

"*Denki, Mamm*." Emily slipped out the door behind her father.

She kept a small garden shed which housed the necessities for her roadside stand, her gardening tools, and farmers market supplies.

"Just one table today, *Dat*. And one chair. Since Susan won't be helping out, I don't think I'll be able to manage more than that." What *had* her older *schweschder* been up to lately, anyhow? No time to ponder that now.

Usually, they set up three tables in a U shape under a white canopy for shade. Since the farmers market closed at noon, they weren't bombarded by the sun's hottest rays, but the blacktop could get pretty hot on the exceptionally warm days.

She grabbed the pretty sign Titus had made for her and her display baskets.

"That's new," *Dat* remarked.

Emily smiled, thinking of her handsome man. "*Jah*, Titus made it for me."

"I see." *Dat* scratched his beard, in thought.

A driver pulled up just then, but not her driver. Her oldest brother Silas stepped out of the vehicle. He frowned when he noticed the farmers market supplies. "Oh no, I forgot about the farmers market," he said.

Emily's brow creased. "What are you talking about, *bruder*?"

"I told Titus Troyer that Shiloh would be able to watch his *kinner* today, but she already had plans. My next thought was you, but the farmers market totally slipped my mind." He slapped his forehead. "Is Susan here?"

"She is now, but she has plans too," Emily glanced at the vehicle. "Are they in the van?"

"*Nee*, at Titus's. I was headed there next."

"Well, I guess you could have the driver drop them off with me at the farmers market." She turned to her father. "We'd better grab a couple extra chairs and the other tables."

Just then, her driver pulled up. They were early. Early was usually a *gut* thing, but not for the farmers market. She wasn't allowed to set up until eight, at the earliest.

Silas frowned. "Are you sure?"

"Well, I don't know how little Benuel will do, but Ty and Rose will be fine. I could actually use a couple of helpers." Emily smiled.

"Okay, great. *Denki, schweschder.*" Silas clapped his hands together once and nodded. "We'll find you there then."

She and *Dat* loaded up her supplies. *Jah*, she'd be early, but she could get her coffee first and take her time setting up her space. It would be fun teaching the *kinner* about the farmers market. Maybe in the future, they could sell there as a family—Titus with his woodworking and Emily with her produce.

She was on her way to a day that promised to be interesting.

Titus thought about canceling his agreement to go to the men's fellowship today, but he hated to inconvenience other people. Especially when they were paying a driver on his behalf. He downed the remainder of his coffee, thinking of his date with Emily last night.

All of a sudden, warmth filled him from the inside out, as he relived the kisses they'd shared at the picnic site. And down by the stream. And in his woodshop. And in his kitchen. And in his sitting room. And in front of her home before he dropped her off in the morning. He released a breath. He wouldn't deny the fact that he wished Emily would have stayed with him until sunrise, but that wouldn't have been appropriate. As it was, their kisses had become quite passionate and he'd had trouble keeping his desires in check. The sooner they wed, the better, in his opinion.

A vehicle pulled up outside. His folks had dropped off the *kinner* about thirty minutes ago. He wasn't sure if Silas had in mind for his *dochder* to come here or if she'd be watching the *kinner* at his house. Truth be told, he was a little worried about Benuel. He wasn't separated from his *dat* very often, and when he was, it was usually with his *grosseldern*. He wasn't sure how he'd do in his absence. Maybe he'd just keep the boy with him today. Sammy Eicher had said there were other *kinner* at the house.

At Silas's knock, he let him inside.

Silas grimaced. "Okay, change of plans. My *dochder* wasn't available today, so I enlisted my baby *schweschder* Emily to help out."

Titus's head snapped up at her name. "Emily?"

"*Jah*. You know who she is, right?"

Titus wanted to laugh, but instead he nodded.

"She's going to be at the farmers market, so we'll need to drop the *kinner* off there. She said she could use extra helpers." Silas eyed him with caution. "Is that okay with you?"

"I'm sure the *kinner* will love being at the farmers market." *And I'll love seeing Emily again.*

"She said she wasn't sure how the youngest one would do, though."

"Not a problem. I planned on keeping Benuel with me."

"Then it sounds like we have everything figured

138

out." Silas looked around. "Are we ready to go?"

"*Jah*. Let me inform the *kinner* of our plans." He nodded toward the vehicle. "We'll be right out."

"Do you have car seats I can help carry?" Silas offered.

"*Jah*. They're in the mudroom. *Denki*."

Emily had barely set up one table, when a white van pulled up. She had trouble containing her smile when her beloved emerged from the vehicle. How she wished just the two of them were the only ones there and they could indulge in a sweet kiss. But that would have to come later.

"We brought your helpers." Titus privily winked at Emily. "Do you need help with anything before we skedaddle?"

Ach, he seemed enthusiastic today. *Gut*. She knew how much her *brieder* enjoyed the men's group. Hopefully, it would be a blessing to Titus as well.

She greeted Rose and Ty, who seemed excited to be there.

Titus came near and began assisting her as she unfolded the next table.

"If you could just help with the canopy, that would be *wunderbaar*," Emily said, pointing to the nylon bag that held it. "I think the *kinner* and I can handle the rest."

When her brothers Silas and Paul jumped out of the van and joined them, the canopy was up in no time. Without even the slightest touch, Titus disappeared with her brothers, leaving her longing for later this evening when they were sure to get in some couple time.

But now, she had a job to do. She turned to her helpers. "Okay, let's put the tablecloths on and get those chairs set up, then the three of us will go hunt down some breakfast."

"We already ate breakfast," Rose said, receiving a nudge from Ty.

"I'm still hungry," Ty said.

"Well, maybe we can find a *little* something to fill your belly, then. Just don't forget that I do have some fruit for us to snack on, too," Emily said.

"I hope it's strawberries."

Emily nodded to Ty. "I did bring a few strawberries."

"Aren't we going to put out the stuff you're selling?" Rose stared at the containers under the table.

"We will when we get back. They don't like us to set up too early. Don't worry, we'll have plenty of time before the customers come." She reached out a hand to each of them and they walked hand-in-hand toward the downtown center square in search of the café.

Emily knew the three of them would be eating much of the profits today, but she was fine with that. Just being out in town with other vendors and enjoying the fresh air and sunshine was enough. And since her special helpers joined her today, she knew they would all have a *wunderbaar* time.

NINETEEN

It wasn't in Titus's nature to seek out friends. He got along with everyone all right, but he often held himself back when it came to relationships outside of family. Family was enough for him. But seeing Silas, Paul, Nathaniel, and Timothy interact in the van had him rethinking his own little bubble.

The four of them were related in a roundabout way. He was an interloper. Of course, when he and Emily married, things would change. He'd become part of their circle as well. Jaden had joined the ranks last year when he'd married Martha.

As soon as the driver came to a stop in front of Sammy's place, Titus unfastened Benuel from his car seat. The boy clung to him, not being familiar with the others in the vehicle. Hopefully, he would interact with the other *kinner* and not cling to him the entire time.

Titus followed the other men as they walked right in to the house, like they lived there. *Ach*, he didn't even do that at his folks' place.

"Welcome!" Sammy's chipper greeting and handshake immediately set his mind at ease. "*Kumm*, grab yourself a cup of coffee and a donut. Miriam and Nora spoiled us today and made up a fresh batch this morning."

He had no clue who Miriam and Nora were, but was grateful for the sweet treats.

Sammy put a hand on his shoulder as they entered the crowded kitchen. "Does everyone know Titus Troyer?"

"Nope." A man near Silas's age, whom he would have characterized as a pretty boy—or someone that turned a lot of ladies' heads—came near and stretched out his hand. "I'm Mike Eicher, Sammy's *gross sohn*. Nice to meet you."

Mike snatched the hand of a woman escaping the kitchen. "And this is my *fraa*, Miri. Miriam."

"*Gut* to meet both of you." Titus smiled, readjusting Benuel on his hip.

"And who is this?" Miriam touched Benuel's hand.

"This is Benuel. He's three," Titus said.

"I bet you'll get along great with Jason. He's three too. Would you like to meet him?" Miriam offered.

Benuel popped his thumb into his mouth and stared at her.

Titus chuckled. "He doesn't talk much."

"I'll be right back," Miriam said, then disappeared from the kitchen.

Another one of the men he didn't know came forward. "I'm Josiah Beachy. Jaden's older brother. And Bailey's father. Do you know who Bailey is?"

"She's friends with Emily Miller, ain't so?"

"Yes. And she's Timothy's *fraa*."

"I confess, I don't know Timothy all that well. I may have seen Bailey before. At the bakery, maybe?"

"Right. She works there with Kayla and Jenny—Silas's and Paul's wives." Josiah glanced around. "And my *fraa* Nora is here somewhere. Likely watching the *kinner*."

"It's nice to meet you, Josiah." He said the name in hopes that he'd remember it.

As Josiah walked off, Miriam returned with a toy clutched in one hand and a young boy holding her other one. "Jason, this is Benuel," her voice was soft as she introduced the youngsters.

Titus crouched down, setting Benuel beside him. "Look, Benuel. Miriam has a toy for you."

Miriam had Jason offer the toy firetruck to Benuel. "Do you want to come play with Jason?"

Benuel eyed Titus.

Titus smiled and nudged him forward. "Go ahead and play. *Dat* isn't going anywhere without you." He pointed to the living room, where the men were gathering. "I'll just be right here."

At Miriam's prompting, Jason reached for Benuel's hand. The three of them walked out of the room. Benuel hadn't even looked back.

Titus sighed in relief, thankful for Miriam's intuitiveness.

"*Kumm*, now," Sammy called all the men to the meeting area. "Let us begin with prayer."

Everyone set their coffee and donuts aside and bowed their heads, but Titus looked up when he realized Sammy intended to pray aloud. A rare thing for the Amish he knew. And since Detweiler's district was even stricter than Bontrager's, Titus guessed it was uncommon here too. But maybe just not so uncommon in this home? He appeared to be the only one surprised.

When Sammy finished, he led the group in introductions. They all told how and if they were related, who their spouse was, and which district they belonged to.

Titus confessed to the group that he was a widower and not related to anyone, for whoever might be unaware.

Sammy's next question took him by surprise, though.

"Let's share where we are. What's on your mind today?" Sammy asked the group. "Since Titus here is new, I'll let him go first."

Titus's face warmed, but at least he could get his part out of the way. His mind immediately went to his intimate moments with Emily. "I've been thinking about remarrying," he admitted.

"Oh, yeah? Who?" Paul Miller asked.

Silas elbowed his younger brother in the gut. "It's none of your business."

"I guess it probably won't be a secret much longer." Titus shrugged. "Emily."

Paul frowned. "Emily who?"

"Miller." Titus chuckled.

"Our baby *schweschder*? Really?" Paul's eyes widened and he shared a look with Silas, then with Jaden Beachy. "I hadn't realized the two of you were dating." Paul's eyes ping-ponged from Silas to Nathaniel. "Did either of you know they were dating?"

"*Nee*. Some of us don't poke our nose into other people's business," Silas said.

"I had an idea because Susan had said something," Nathaniel said. "But when Titus and his *kinner* came for supper, I figured that was what was going on."

"We haven't told anyone yet, and we don't have a date set, so I'd appreciate it if this stays between us," Titus folded his hands in his lap.

"Oh, boy," Paul said. "So, our folks don't know yet?"

"*Nee.* Nobody. We actually just discussed it last night. Which is why it's on my mind." He glanced at Sammy. "That's kind of why I wanted to keep it a secret."

"Your secrets are safe here," Sammy assured.

"Well, I'm happy for you." *Jaden Beachy was happy for him?*

"So am I," Nathaniel said.

Titus shook his head in gratefulness. "*Denki.*"

All in all, the men's fellowship had gone well for both Titus and Benuel. His son didn't want to leave when the time came, which meant he'd enjoyed himself. Titus felt comfortable around these men now. Even the initial awkwardness between him and Jaden Beachy had vanished, especially when he admitted wanting to marry Emily Miller. If that happened, Titus would become a brother-in-law to half of the men in the fellowship group. He wouldn't just gain a *wunderbaar fraa*, he'd gain a whole new family.

He loved the camaraderie between Emily's brothers, and the friendship they had with the other men in the group. He was looking forward to learning more about each of them. He'd heard bits and pieces of their stories, which had piqued his curiosity.

Since he only had one sister, being around males never really came naturally to him. His family had definitely been one of their community's smallest. His mother had complications during labor with his sister, so his folks had opted for permanent surgery. Not something common among the Amish, but not totally unheard of either. Most would continue creating *kinner* and leave the results up to *Gott*. But his father couldn't stand the thought of losing his *mamm*—something Titus understood very well. His folks had never talked about how the community reacted to their decision, although he was quite certain some folks would have the opinion that they had played *Gott* by not allowing His will to prevail, since *Der Herr* was the Creator and the Taker of life.

For himself, he didn't know where he stood on the matter. Honestly, he understood and agreed with both sides to some extent. And he wasn't sure what decision he would make, if he and his *fraa* were in the same predicament. But he would hold no judgement against anyone who had to make such a difficult decision. Judgement belonged to *Der Herr*.

TWENTY

It was close to eleven thirty when Titus's driver pulled up to the farmers market. Fortunately, everyone, including their driver, wanted to stroll the farmers market. Emily's *bruder* Paul opted to watch her booth for her while they perused the other vendor booths. Titus was just happy to see Emily and the *kinner*.

The boys were fast asleep under Emily's canopy. Benuel had conked out in the van, so Titus carefully transferred him to the quilt Ty was sleeping on. Rose stayed behind to help Paul with prices.

Titus had been tempted to take Emily's hand, as they walked side-by-side down the street.

"How did the men's fellowship go?" She glanced his way.

"*Gut.* We can talk about it later. How'd your booth do?"

"Not as good as I thought." She frowned. "Perhaps one of the stores is having a strawberry sale this week."

"Maybe. But store-bought aren't half as *gut* as yours. Straight from the farm is always best. Especially since yours are so sweet and juicy." He shook his head. "And they're organic too, ain't so? So they don't carry that sulfuric taste."

"You taste that too?" Her jaw dropped. "I thought I was the only one."

"You could bring some store-bought strawberries, so people could taste the difference, or—" He stopped and stared at her. "You know what you need? You need to make up some of your strawberry shortcake and give samples away. You could even give a copy of your recipe to your customers who buy a certain amount."

"Titus! That's a really *gut* idea! I love it!"

And *he* loved the smile she graced him with.

"What do you think of coming out here with me and selling some of your wood projects? Or your eggs?"

He rubbed his beard. *Not eggs.* "I'm not sure. Do you think the *Englisch* would like my wood stuff? It's not too fancy."

"I think that jewelry box you made me was pretty fancy." She grinned at him again. "I put our rings in there, by the way."

"You did? *Gut*."

"Do you think you could make one for Bailey? I'd love to give her one as a gift. She has a cute necklace and other things her *dat* bought her when he was *Englisch*. I'd pay you for it, of course."

Titus chuckled. "We're to be married soon. I'm not going to charge you."

"I want you to. I want the gift to be from me, not you."

"Have it your way, then. Not sure I understand the way a woman's mind works." He laughed.

"I don't think most men do, but that's okay. We don't get you, either."

He walked up to one of the booths selling flowers. "Please give me the largest bouquet you have."

The vendor smiled and handed him a bunch of colorful blossoms of various kinds. She told him the price. He paid, then handed the bouquet to Emily.

"Titus! Did you really just pay forty dollars for this?" They made their way back to Emily's booth.

"Don't worry about the price. Just enjoy them."

"I'd kiss you, if we weren't in public."

"And I'd kiss you back." He winked.

"You're spoiling me again."

"I can't help it. I'm in love with you, Emily Miller."

"Your room is beginning to look like a gift shop," Susan remarked as she poked her head into Emily's bedroom.

Emily sighed in contentment. "I know. Titus spoils me."

"It's a waste." Susan shook her head in disapproval.

"Are you jealous?"

Susan snorted. "Whatever."

"It's only a waste when it's spent on someone who doesn't appreciate them," Emily quipped. "This is how Titus shows his love. It isn't wasted on me."

Susan rolled her eyes, then stormed off.

Again, Emily wondered about her *schweschder*. She seemed so discontent lately. Perhaps Emily needed to pray for her more.

"Emily," Nathaniel's voice called from downstairs. "Something came for you."

She peeked out the window to see a brown delivery truck heading down the road. What on earth? She hadn't ordered anything.

Emily hurried downstairs. A small box sat on the table.

"What is it? What did you order?" Nathaniel asked.

"Nothing. I have no idea what it could be." She shrugged.

"Well, it's got your name on it. Open it."

"Okay." She cautiously opened the box. "They're business cards! *Ach*, they're so cute. Look at this." She turned it over and showed it to Nathaniel. "It's my recipe for strawberry shortcake."

Nathaniel examined it, squinting. "*Jah*, but you need a magnifying glass to read it." He chuckled.

"Titus is such a sweetheart." She was tempted to swoon again. "He does so much for me."

"I think he's lost his mind."

She slapped Nathaniel's arm with the packaging slip. "He loves me, that's all."

"*Jah*, well, I've never done anything like that for a girl."

"Which may be why you're still unmarried," she teased.

"That was low, Emily." He shook his head, laughing.

Squeaky brakes drew their attention outside.

"You're kidding me," Nathaniel said. "The delivery guy's back."

Emily walked outside.

"Is there an Emily Miller here?"

"That's me." She smiled.

"Sorry, I forgot this one earlier." He handed her a package. "I believe that's all for today."

"Thank you!" she called as he headed back toward his vehicle.

Nathaniel appeared at her side. "Alright, let's see what else Dr. Love got for you."

Emily pushed his arm, before taking her box inside. This one was larger and more square than the last one had been. She sighed as she ran her hand over the box.

"Well, you going to open it or gawk at it all day?"

"You're more excited than I am about it."

"I don't think that's possible." He handed her his pocket knife.

"You're right." She slid his knife under the packaging tape, then carefully removed the abundance of packing peanuts.

Nathaniel took one and batted it with his hand.

She shook a finger at her older brother. "If you make a mess, you're cleaning it up."

"I'll blame it on you." He chuckled, then began juggling the packing peanuts. "Hurry up, already."

Finally, she pulled out two fancy drinking glasses in her special color. Tears pricked her eyes. She turned to Nathaniel and shook her head, unable to speak any words.

Nathaniel whistled. "Wow, those are...nice. Dr. Love doesn't mess around, does he?"

With her heart full, Emily took her treasures up to

her room. What would it be like to be married to this *wunderbaar* man who seemed to be able to read her so intimately?

TWENTY-ONE

Tonight was the night Emily and Titus planned to share their news with her family over supper. Tomorrow night, they'd share it with his. They planned to set a date after speaking with them. They'd both agreed that they didn't want to wait till the wedding season this fall.

Titus's hands became clammy, anticipating looks of disapproval that were sure to come his way. He had to remind himself to breathe. It would have been less nerve wracking if he'd brought the *kinner* along, but they'd thought it best to leave them with his folks.

They wanted to talk to the *kinner* privately after they spoke with each set of parents. After all, this decision would change *all* their lives. He was quite certain the *kinner* would be thrilled with Emily becoming their new *mamm*.

Emily met him at the hitching post with a couple

of books under her arm. She was her usually bubbly self, but she seemed extra excited this evening. "*Mamm* and I went to the library today. I checked out some books that I think will help Benuel."

He nodded. He was too nervous to share her excitement over books, but appreciated the gesture. "That's *gut*. We'll have to look over them later."

What he really needed right now was long hard kiss to release some his pent-up energy, but it didn't look like he'd be getting a kiss till later. But maybe...he glanced around. "Where is everyone?"

"They're inside waiting for us."

He took the books from her hand and set them in his buggy. "May I have a minute?"

She nodded, a question in her eyes.

He pulled her just into the barn, lifted his hand to her face, dropped his lips to hers, and drank in everything Emily. His tension melted away like the snow at sunrise. If only they weren't on a time schedule.

He groaned when they parted. "I needed that so much." His thumb grazed her lips as he pondered ditching their dinner plans and taking her home. He shook his head, to bring him back to reality.

"We better go in now." She breathed out the words. "Is my *kapp* on straight?"

"It looks *gut*." His gaze roamed her attire. "You look *gut*."

Her cheeks darkened at his compliment.

"*Denki* for all my gifts. My *schweschder* says I'm becoming a spoiled brat." Emily laughed.

"Spoiled? Maybe. Brat? Never." He smiled as they stepped into the house.

❧

"Emily tells us the two of you wanted to discuss something," *Mamm* prodded Titus.

Titus glanced across the table at Emily. He looked like he was trying to muster a smile. *Ach*, the poor guy was nervous. Her heart went out to him. It probably didn't help that Susan had been glaring at him earlier.

Emily nodded, encouraging him to speak.

"We want to get hitched." His words rushed out of his mouth. He quickly took a drink of water, staring deeply into the glass.

"We were thinking before the wedding season," Emily added.

Mamm gasped. "Before the wedding season?" She frowned at Emily and shook her head. "*Nee*, dochder. That is too soon."

"I agree," *Dat* chimed in. "You two haven't even been courting long. You need time to get to know

161

each other better."

Titus met her eyes and shrugged.

"There is no need to rush things, *dochder*." *Mamm* stopped and stared at her. "Or is there?" She frowned at Titus.

"*Nee*," she and Titus said simultaneously.

"Oh, *gut*," *Mamm* released a breath, putting her hand over her heart. "After Martha..." She seemed to realize what she was about to say, then clamped her lips tight.

"We can wait until the early wedding season, *jah*?" Titus lifted a brow, finally finding his voice again.

"I guess. If everyone thinks it will be better." Emily relented. It was only a few extra months. They could be patient if they had to.

Mamm nodded. "It will be better for everyone all around. Preparing for a wedding is no small thing."

"I'm so glad it's over," Titus admitted. He took a breath once they were outside in the fresh air. "I don't know if I've ever been more nervous in my life."

Emily slipped her hand into his. "Not even at your first wedding?"

"Well, maybe. But it's been a long time."

"You did fine," she assured him.

He laughed. "I said like two words."

"It was more than two." She squeezed his hand. "The important part is that they didn't reject the idea."

"*Jah*. You don't mind waiting?"

"*Nee*. I mean, it'll be hard, but *nee*. We'll have our whole lives together, ain't so?"

Our whole lives. But how long would that be? He always thought he'd grow old and gray with Helen at his side, but alas, here he was in his thirties contemplating remarriage. How many *fraas* would he go through before he made it to the end of his life?

He couldn't stand to think about it. He would not lose Emily too. Not if it was in his power. He hadn't done enough for Helen. He wouldn't make the same mistake with Emily.

"Remember, I'm picking you up early tomorrow."

"Right. So I can help Rose make strawberry shortcake to take to your *mamm's*. I haven't forgotten."

"You know, she glows when she's around you." He kissed her forehead. "I can't wait to talk to the *kinner* about us. I think Rose and Ty might almost be as excited as I am."

"I still can't believe the five of us will be a family soon. It almost seems too *gut* to be true."

It almost seems too gut *to be true.* Emily's words echoed in Titus's head. Threatening him. Mocking him. He attempted to drown the words out, but they persisted.

Nee, nothing was going to happen to his precious Emily.

TWENTY-TWO

*E*mily stared into Titus's extra refrigerator, her brow lowered, mouth open. "Rose...why do you have all these eggs in here?"

"*Dat* says we can't run out."

Emily scratched her head, still puzzled. "But this *entire* fridge is full of eggs."

"We have them every day," Rose reasoned.

"But you don't need *this* many. *Nobody* needs this many."

"It has to stay full. *Dat* says so. If there is more than that, we sell them or give them away. But there can't be less."

Emily stared at Rose. "Why?"

Rose shrugged. "I don't know. It's just what *Dat* says."

"I don't understand this." She stared at the dozens upon dozens of eggs, trying to make sense of what her eyes were seeing.

"Ask *Dat*."

"*Jah*, I think I will." Emily closed the refrigerator door and frowned. Surely there was a *gut* explanation.

A half hour had passed. The dessert was nearly ready. Finally, Titus and the boys made their way into the house.

"Hurry and wash up, *buwe*. We're going to your *grosseldern* soon." Titus winked at Emily. "Be back in a jiffy."

He handed Rose a few cartons of eggs. "You know what to do with those." Then he disappeared from the kitchen.

So, apparently she wouldn't be talking to him about the excess eggs. If that was even the proper word. Because what this family kept went *way* beyond excess.

"I'm planning on sharing our news with Bailey tomorrow." Emily smiled at Titus as he drove her home. She still hadn't mentioned the egg thing to him, but she didn't want to while the *kinner* were in ear shot.

"Is that so?" Titus smiled. "Where will you see her?"

"I'm planning to drive to my *bruder's* bakery, where she works."

"With who?"

She shrugged. "No one. Just by myself."

Titus frowned. Why was he frowning?

"Do you not want me to tell her yet?"

"*Nee.* I don't want you driving to the bakery by yourself."

"What do you mean?"

"Just what I said." He glanced at her. "I'll take you. What time do you want to go?"

"Titus, I don't need you to take me. I can drive myself."

"*Nee.*"

Emily rubbed her forehead, then look at the *kinner* in the back. All of them had fallen asleep.

She lowered her voice. "Titus, I'm not going to stop driving by myself. I've been driving by myself for many years yet."

"But I want you to. I insist. Just let me take you."

"Titus, it's ridiculous for you to come all the way over here to take me to the bakery, when I live just down the road." She shook her head. "Besides, I want to speak with Bailey alone. We haven't had a chance to talk in a while."

"I can wait in the buggy."

"Titus, no."

"You don't want me to go with you, then?" He maneuvered the buggy into the driveway.

"*Nee*, it's not that. It's just that sometimes I like to do things on my own."

"Why?" He challenged.

"I just do. Why not?"

"You're being stubborn."

"No, I'm not. I'm being completely rational. It is a normal thing to want to go somewhere by yourself."

"I can't keep you safe if you're not with me."

Emily stared at him. "Keep me safe? That's not within your power."

"*Jah*, it is if you're in my buggy." He pulled up to the hitching post.

It *finally* dawned on her and her heart ached for him. Her frustration eased just a bit. "Is this because your first *fraa* died in a buggy accident?"

He nodded. "If I would have been driving, it never would have happened."

"You don't know that." She covered his hand with hers as sympathy filled her.

"*Jah*, I do." He pressed his lips together. "I won't make the same mistake twice. I wouldn't be able to live with myself if the same thing happened to you."

"Titus." She reached over and touched his cheek.

"I get it, *schatzi*. I understand how you feel."

"Then you agree?"

"No, I don't. I can't. I'm sorry." She dropped her hand.

He stared at her. "But you'll obey me in this when we're married?"

Ach. She felt a headache coming on.

She stared at Titus as they sat in his buggy. In the quiet night. With the little ones sleeping in the back. Her lips pulled downward. She didn't want to speak the words, but managed to force them out anyhow. "Is this...is this a deal breaker?"

He grimaced, then nodded once.

Emily's chin trembled thinking of what this meant. Could she abide by Titus's wishes and *never* drive anywhere by herself? *Nee*, she couldn't even abide the thought. Of being imprisoned in her own home. Of not being able to take a simple trip to her *bruder's* store. Of not being allowed to visit her loved ones at will. A prisoner. That was exactly how she'd feel if she didn't have the freedom to do those things.

She loved Titus and his *kinner*. Truly. But...

"Then, I guess—" She couldn't help the rush of tears. Because she knew there was no way she could agree to Titus's unfathomable demands. "I guess the deal's off."

She scurried from the buggy, then ran into the house and up to her room before he could see the first tears fall.

Titus sat dumbfounded. Had his request really been *that* unreasonable? Not to his thinking. He had to protect his own. And he couldn't do that if they weren't with him.

He'd failed to protect Helen and look what happened. *He* should have been the one to go fetch the eggs. *He* should have been the one in that buggy. *He* should have had enough laying hens so a trip down the road wouldn't have been necessary. His *fraa's* death was his fault, plain and simple.

He refused to lose another *fraa*. He couldn't go through that again. Especially losing someone like sweet Emily. It was better to let her go now, than to lose her forever.

At least, that was what he told himself.

TWENTY-THREE

)t had been three weeks since they'd called the wedding off. Three weeks since Titus had attended the men's fellowship. Three weeks since his world came crashing down. Again.

But there was nothing he could do about it. If Emily wanted to live her life without him, then he wouldn't stop her.

During church on Sunday, he'd glanced at the women once, but she hadn't been sitting among them. However, he'd received a glare from her *schweschder* Susan. She'd never seemed to like him in the first place.

He now stared at the box, in the corner of the dining room, mocking him. The sum of everything he'd given to Emily, including his heart. She'd sent it back last week. He hadn't opened it—he hadn't needed to. The moment it showed up, he knew. He wasn't quite sure what to do with it, so he'd left it there.

"*Dat*, when is Emily coming over again? She hasn't been here in forever," Rose said as she poured him his morning coffee.

He hadn't told his *kinner*, but he knew they suspected something since Emily hadn't been over to visit them and vice versa.

"I don't think Emily is going to come back, *dochder*." He didn't even bother with the peppermint patty today. What was the use, anyway? It wouldn't bring joy back to his heart.

"Why not? I thought you and Emily were going to get hitched. I thought we were going to get a new *mamm*." Rose's voice shook and he longed to comfort her.

"*Nee*. Not this time."

"But we love Emily and she loves us!" Tears ran down Rose's cheeks, but Titus was helpless to stop them. "Why can't you marry her, *Dat*?"

"You wouldn't understand."

"It's because of your stupid eggs, isn't it?"

"You know you're not allowed to say that word," Titus warned. "And it has nothing to do with the eggs."

"Yes, it does. You care more about those eggs than

you do Emily!" She scowled at him. *Ach*, when had his *dochder* ever done that?

"You will not speak to me in that tone." His voice was firm.

Rose let out a cry, then rushed out of the room.

"*Ach*, what have I done now?" he whispered to the stale air.

Having been abandoned by Rose, his eggs sizzled on the stove. He'd have to finish cooking breakfast this morning. *And what a* wunderbaar *morning it was shaping up to be!* He couldn't stop his sarcastic thought. And he wasn't going to bother apologizing to *Der Herr* for his ungrateful attitude, either.

After Titus had dropped Rose off at school, he instructed the boys to go play in their room. He needed some time alone to gather his thoughts. The floral perfume he'd purchased for Emily during one of his shopping excursions still sat on his nightstand. He'd ignored the strange looks he received when he purchased it at the store. A man should be able to buy women's perfume if he wanted to.

Had he given it to Emily, he suspected it would be in that box by the mudroom. Which reminded him... He quickly fetched the box, brought it back to his room, and shoved it under his bed. He hadn't decided what to do with it yet, but at least now it wouldn't be staring at him every time he sat at the table.

When he entered the kitchen again, a knock sounded at the door. He glanced through the glass. *Ach*, Sammy Eicher. What was the older man doing way out here? *And with his buggy?*

Titus opened the door and invited him in.

"Missed you at the men's fellowship the past few weeks," Sammy remarked.

Jah, he probably wouldn't be going back. "Been busy." Titus lied. Unless "busy moping" qualified.

"I see." Sammy glanced around. "The *kinner* at school?"

"Just Rose is old enough for school. Ty will start next year. The boys are in their room." He needed to distract himself. "Uh, would you like some coffee?"

"I'd love some. I'd even be inclined to try one of them fancy peppermints you're so fond of." Sammy raised his bushy eyebrows.

"Where do you work, *sohn*?"

Titus scratched his beard, then joined Sammy at the table with two mugs of coffee and two peppermint patties. "I *chust* work at home right now. Since my *fraa* passed, I've been home with the *kinner*. We actually had a small life insurance policy on both of us, so I haven't needed any extra income. When all of the *kinner* are in school, I'll probably take a job."

"I see." Sammy sipped his coffee. "Tell me about your *fraa.*"

There was something about this older man that set his mind at ease. Like he could confide in him about anything.

He raised a half smile. "She was a *wunderbaar* woman—a *wunderbaar fraa*. Would do anything I asked. Loved the *kinner.*"

"Was she a believer in Jesus?"

"She talked about *Der Herr* quite a bit." He nodded. "I think so."

"How about you?" Sammy seemed to look straight through him.

Titus shook his head. "I really don't know anymore."

Sadness seemed to enter Sammy's eyes. "What makes you say that?"

"I'm beginning to realize that I'm a failure, Sammy. At everything." As he said the words, his heart squeezed, like it was a piece of wood held tight by the metal clamps he used in his woodshop.

"I don't think that's true, *sohn.*"

"It is." He forbade his tears from falling. "I couldn't even protect my *fraa*. It was *my* responsibility to keep her safe. *I'm* the one who

175

should have been driving the buggy."

"You said it was an accident. You can't control accidents." Sammy frowned.

"I shouldn't have let her drive. If we would have had laying hens, she wouldn't have needed to go fetch eggs." He stared at Sammy. "Why did I even want eggs for breakfast? I didn't need them. She could have made pancakes or oatmeal. But no, I wanted eggs."

Sammy listened quietly as Titus prattled on nonsensically.

"There are so many things I could have done differently. Should have done differently. Then my *fraa* would still be alive." He shoved away a tear.

"Didn't you say you were thinking of remarrying?"

He grimaced. "*Jah*. But *nee*. We called it off."

"Why?" Sammy's hands cradled his coffee mug.

"Because she insists on driving by herself. And I won't lose another *fraa*. I won't, Sammy."

"And you think her driving alone will result in her death?"

He nodded. "I know it will. *Der Herr* is against me."

"*Der Herr* is not against you."

"Then explain why my first *fraa* is *dot*."

"I do not know the reason. But I do know that we all must face death someday. None of us knows when that day will be. Unless we are here when Christ returns." He smiled at that last part.

"Why do we have to die?"

"Well, technically, we don't." Sammy chuckled.

"But you just said—"

"I know. But if we are believers, we are only exchanging our old bodies for new ones. If we are absent from the body, we are present with *Der Herr*. We are alive for eternity."

"I'm not sure how all that works."

"Simply put, if your *fraa* was a believer, she's happier now with Jesus than she could ever be with you."

"You keep saying *if* she was a *believer*. Isn't *everyone* a believer?"

"*Nee*. There are very few in this world that are true believers. Consider the words of *Der Herr*, '*Enter ye in at the strait gate: for wide is the gate, and broad is the way, that leadeth to destruction, and many there be which go in thereat: Because strait is the gate, and narrow is the way, which leadeth unto life, and few there be that find it.*' Jesus also said, '*Not every one that saith unto me, Lord, Lord, shall enter into the kingdom of heaven; but he that doeth the will of my Father which is in heaven. Many will say to me in that day, Lord, Lord, have we not prophesied in thy name?*

and in thy name cast out devils? And in thy name done many wonderful works? And then will I profess unto them, I never knew you: depart from me, ye that work iniquity.' You see? We must know Him. *He* must know us."

"How can He know us? How can we know Him?" He rubbed his head.

Sammy explained, "When a person trusts Christ as their Saviour, He sends His Holy Ghost to live inside them. As that person reads and studies *Gott's* Word, he learns *Der Herr's* will for his life. The Holy Ghost will guide him, and He'll let that person know when he is pleasing *Gott* or not."

"I'm not making the connection. What do being a believer and knowing have to do with one another?"

"When we place our faith in Jesus—allowing His blood to wash away our sins—it must be a heart belief. It can't *chust* be intellectual. Because when Christ enters your heart, He changes you. He places new desires in your heart. He gives you the power to overcome your struggles and temptations and fears." Sammy stared straight at him now. "And it sounds like you have some of those in your life."

Ach, Sammy was right.

"If you call out to *Der Herr* and place your trust in Him, He will comfort you and give you the strength you need to overcome your fears. Gott *is our refuge and strength, a very present help in trouble. Therefore will not we fear...*" Sammy continued, "Remember that the spirit of fear does not come from *Der Herr. For* Gott *hath not given us a spirit of fear, but of power, of love, and of a sound mind.* Fear is from the enemy and he does his best to trip us up with it. And let me say that he is mighty *gut* at what he does."

Was this fear he was holding onto? The eggs, keeping the *kinner* close, driving alone...losing someone dear to him? Again.

Jah, it's the truth, he realized. It was his fear that had come between him and Emily. It was his fear that had caused the rift between him and his *dochder*. It was his fear that had come between him and *Der Herr.* Truth be told, it was taking over his life.

Even Rose perceived it.

"You are right, Sammy. It is fear that is ruining my life. But I feel powerless against it," Titus admitted. "What should I do?"

"Call out to Jesus. Repent of your lack of faith and ask Him to save you. Ask Him for His help. He will give you the victory. He will provide the strength you need to overcome. He will renew and restore the relationships in your life. *If* you let Him." Sammy reached for his hand across the table, then bowed his head. "Dear *Gott*, my friend Titus here is in need of Your help. Please take his hand and help him. Show him that he doesn't have to do it alone. Show him his need for You. Show him how much You love him. Amen."

When Sammy lifted his head, tears shimmered in his eyes. "The rest is up to you, *sohn*."

Titus nodded and bowed his head. In silence, he poured out his heart to *Der Herr*. As he prayed and confessed each fear and failure, a burden seemed to lift from his shoulders. The weight of guilt had disappeared. He physically felt lighter when he finished his prayer.

He released a long breath and stared at Sammy in amazement. "Wow. For the first time, I feel like I actually connected with *Gott*."

"Isn't it awesome?" Sammy's eyes shined with joy.

"*Jah*, for sure."

"*Chust* remember, if you ever doubt *Gott's* love for you, go back to the cross. There is no greater love than that."

"I will." Titus stood. "Sammy, are you hungry for some eggs?"

"I can always eat." Sammy grinned.

Titus went to his extra fridge. "Do you need any eggs? I need to clear these out."

"I suppose we can always use eggs. Miriam will appreciate it." Sammy scratched his chin. "But let me pay you for them."

"*Nee*, I need to give these away." Titus waved his arm to beckon Sammy. "*Kumm*, here."

Sammy stood next to him staring into the refrigerator. "That's a lot of eggs."

"That's my fear."

Sammy's brow lowered. "You're scared of eggs?"

Titus chuckled. "*Nee*. The morning my *fraa* died, she'd gone out to fetch some eggs from one of the families in the *g'may*. For my breakfast."

"I see. So, if you kept enough eggs on hand at all times, no one would ever need to fetch any." Wow, Sammy hit the nail on the head.

"That was my thought."

"And now?"

"Now, I feel like I need to get rid of them. Not all of them, *chust* most. I'll keep a couple dozen." Titus turned to Sammy. "Do you know of anyone who could use eggs?"

"I imagine Jenny Miller uses a lot at the bakery."

"That's perfect." Titus smiled. "And what about a refrigerator? Do you know of anyone who could use a fridge?"

Sammy shook his head. "You know. Funniest

thing. Silas was *chust* telling me about someone's refrigerator going out *chust* this morning. Isn't *Der Herr gut*?"

"So *gut*."

TWENTY-FOUR

"*E*mily!" *Mamm's* voice called from downstairs.
Hair still down, Emily stepped out of her
room and walked to the top of the stairs. "I
thought you didn't need help with breakfast this
morning."

"*Nee*, it's not that. There's a box here for you."

"A box?" Emily frowned.

The last time a box had come for her, it had been
from Titus. Sorrow once again crushed her heart.
How she missed being with him and the *kinner*. The
thought of living without them *almost* drove her to
agreeing to Titus's unreasonable demands. But she
had to stand her ground. She knew she wouldn't be
happy without her freedom.

"*Dat* said he'll bring it up," *Mamm* called back.

A moment later, *Dat* carried a very familiar looking
box to her bedroom.

"*Ach*, that's the stuff I sent back to Titus." Emily sighed.

"It says 'Return to Sender.' But it looks like there's a note attached," *Dat* said. "Well, I'll leave you to it."

She watched as her father disappeared, then closed the door to her room. She stared at the box, wondering what it could mean.

Emily unfolded the note and silently read the words. *Need help cleaning out egg fridge today. If interested, apply at the Troyer household.* Come alone.

She reread the words, then laughed. She turned the note over and found something else. *P.S. Peppermint coffee available. I love you.*

Emily opened her door. "*Mamm*, I can't go shopping with you today after all. I need to help clean out a refrigerator."

Mamm appeared at the bottom of the stairs. "You'd rather clean out a refrigerator, than go shopping? Who are you and what have you done with my *dochder*?"

Emily jogged downstairs and handed *Mamm* the note.

"I see." *Mamm* sighed. "I guess I'll *chust* have to go shopping alone, then."

"I'll go with you, *schatzi*," *Dat* said over *Mamm's* shoulder.

"You always want to buy things we don't need," *Mamm* contended. "I spend twice as much when you come along."

"Well, you better get used to it, *fraa*. By the look of things, it doesn't look like you'll have a shopping partner much longer." *Dat* winked at Emily.

Although Titus had left that note, Emily still wasn't certain what it meant exactly. Other than the obvious. He was cleaning out his egg fridge. But he'd asked her to come *alone*, which meant... *Nee*, she wouldn't get her hopes up. But just the fact that he specifically said he wanted her to come alone implied that she would be driving by herself.

She guided her father's mare into the Troyers' driveway and stopped in front of the hitching post. She stepped down and tethered the horse.

Titus exited his woodshop, clad in attire totally inappropriate for cleaning out a fridge. He was wearing his favorite color shirt and his *for gut* clothes, including his black felt hat. *Ach*, he looked so handsome.

As Titus neared, Emily noticed there was something different about him—other than his fancy clothes, that was. His entire face seemed to shine. His eyes, usually dull, were bright and hopeful. She could feel joy just being in his presence. It radiated from him.

And that was when she knew.

This wasn't about eggs, or cleaning out a fridge, or driving alone. Titus had changed. He'd become a new man.

"Did you come to fill the position?" Titus teased.

"I did." Emily smiled.

"I'm sorry, it's already been filled."

She frowned. "What?"

"Sammy Eicher helped me clean it out earlier. Said he knew of someone who could use it."

"Oh." She frowned. "Then why did I come?"

"Well, you see, I have this other position that needs to be filled, too." His eyes bore into hers and he took a step closer. "And Sammy Eicher *chust* doesn't meet the criteria."

"What is the criteria?" She swallowed as he took another step closer.

"Well, this position can only be filled by a female." His eyes did a once-over.

Emily found her cheeks warm all of a sudden. "I see. And what does this female need to do?"

"Well, she'll have to know how to drive a buggy. Because I'd need her to take the *kinner* to school and pick them up every day." He stepped closer, causing

Emily's heart to pound. "That is, until they're old enough to drive themselves."

"What else will she need to do?" She blinked.

"Since we're talking about school, she'll have to accompany the *kinner* and me tonight. It's Rose's last day of the year and they have some special goings-on."

Emily nodded. "I think she can do that. Was there something else?"

"Well, she'll have to know how to make a really *gut* strawberry shortcake, you see, because the *kinner* love strawberry shortcake." He smirked. "And then there's the last qualification."

"What's that?"

He took one final step and lifted his hand to her cheek. "Peppermint coffee kisses. It is an absolute must that she enjoy those."

Emily licked her lips in anticipation of his kiss. "I...I think I might qualify for the position."

"*Gut.* Because I didn't want to have to look for anyone else." He lowered his head, and ever so gently swept his lips over hers.

Emily suddenly pushed back, her heart still pounding from Titus's kiss. "Wait. I have a requirement too."

Titus hitched an eyebrow, amusement sparkling in his eyes. "That so?"

She nodded. "Must love cats."

He chuckled. "I'd love anything in order to get another one of those kisses from you."

Emily's heart soared as her fingers wrapped around his suspender and she tugged him close. His lips met hers again, and she couldn't help but dream of the *wunderbaar* future she'd have with her beloved.

EPILOGUE

Winter, the following year...

Titus and Emily Troyer strolled down the baking aisle of the local grocery store in search of ingredients for a new strawberry recipe Emily had stumbled upon. While she didn't have any fresh berries, she'd preserved plenty from their summer harvest this year.

She and Titus had expanded production, and their entire family, including five-year-old Benuel, helped out on the farm. Benuel's speech had improved greatly since their wedding last year and continued. She figured that by the time he was ready to start school, he should be on par with the other *kinner*. And, if he wasn't, that was okay too.

Rose and Ty both excelled in school—Rose in her studies, and Ty on the playground. Rose also expanded her sewing skills to include trousers for her *brieder*. She and Emily had modeled her latest matching dresses for the men of the family just yesterday.

Emily loved her ready-made family more than her heart could contain. Which reminded her…"I need to go fetch something. I'll be right back." She left Titus standing near the checkout. "Go ahead and start ringing it up," she told him.

A minute later, she returned to the line.

"What did you get?" Titus eyed her curiously.

"It's a surprise." She winked, holding the item behind her back.

He chuckled and shook his head. "Peppermint patties?"

Emily kept her secretive smile to herself, but placed the item she'd fetched on the conveyer belt at the last minute, out of Titus's view.

Having placed all the items in shopping bags, the cashier rung up their order and told Titus the total. He paid, and they carried their groceries to their waiting vehicle.

"What are hiding from me, *fraa*?" Titus's eyes sparkled with mirth.

"You'll see soon enough. But you'll need patience."

"You know I'm not *gut* with that." He raised a

brow, then attempted to look into her bag.

"You're worse than Ty sometimes." She swatted his hand away.

⁕

Titus tapped his foot as he waited for his *fraa*. He'd already put on a pot of water for coffee and stoked the fire. Emily's folks had kept the *kinner* tonight, so they could enjoy a little alone time. But Titus expected his wife to be included in the alone time.

Finally, she ambled into the room. *Ach*, did she have tears in her eyes?

"*Schatzi*, what's wrong?" He frowned.

She pulled something from behind her back and set it in his hands. "I'm sick."

He stared down at a plastic device, expecting to see her temperature displayed. But this wasn't a thermometer at all. Then it dawned on him.

"You're sick?"

Twin tears rushed down her cheeks.

"But this...this is a *gut* sick, ain't not?"

She nodded and he pulled her onto his lap.

He lifted her chin. "We're going to have a *boppli*, *jah*?"

"*Jah*."

"*Ach*, Emily! This is the best news ever! Not that

you're sick, but that we're going to have a baby. You're happy, aren't you?"

"I'm very happy. That's why I'm crying."

"I thought you were crying because you're sick." He brushed a tear away with the pad of his thumb.

"*Jah*, that too."

Seven months later...

Titus left the bedroom so "his three girls" could have some time together, he'd said.

"*Ach*, she's such a precious *boppli*!" Rose held her baby *schweschder*. "Can we give her a name?"

"What should we call her?" Emily asked, loving the bonding between sisters her eyes were beholding.

"What about..." Rose bit her fingernail.

"Go ahead," Emily encouraged.

"I was thinking maybe Helen, after our first *mamm*?"

"*Ach*, Rose, that's perfect!"

"Do you think so? You think *Dat* will like it?"

"I think he'll love it." She gestured toward the door. "Let's ask him."

Rose called Titus into the room.

"We've thought of a name for her," Emily smiled.

The look of love reflected in Titus's eyes. "Already?"

Emily shared a glance with their oldest *dochder*. "The first name was Rose's idea and I think it's *wunderbaar*."

"What is it?" Titus glanced at Rose.

"Helen Rose Troyer," Emily announced.

Tears shimmered in Rose's eyes. "Rose? After me, too?"

"I think it's perfect," Titus grinned.

"*Der Herr* is perfect," Emily whispered.

He stepped near and kissed his *fraa* on the lips. "Indeed, He is."

THE END

Dear Reader,

Did you enjoy Titus and Emily's story?

Some of Titus's character was based on a young Amish man that I know of, my friend's daughter's beau. He isn't a widower, but he is a giver and loves to spoil his intended. My jaw dropped when I saw all the fun gifts he'd showered her with, and I admit that I was a little envious! She's definitely the apple of his eye.

You don't expect something like that with the Amish, do you? I know I didn't. It's nice to know that there are still some romantic men out there—even Amish ones.

Titus also struggled with fear, or more accurately, a phobia. Phobia is different than fear. A phobia is an irrational fear.

We've seen quite a bit of fear, and fear-driven decisions, over the past year on a global scale.

Fear can be dangerous. It can cripple us and cause us to do irrational things. We must realize that fear is one of the enemy's tactics to immobilize us and make us ineffective for the cause of Christ. We must not let it control our thoughts or our lives. We must remember that **God is in control at all times**.

The theme of this book can be found in Psalm 46:1-2b. I encourage you to memorize it. *"GOD is our refuge and strength, a very present help in trouble. Therefore will not we fear..."*

Let God be your everything, including your victory over fear.

Blessings in Christ,
Jennifer Spredemann

Thanks for reading!
Word of mouth is one of the best forms of advertisement and a HUGE blessing to the author. If you enjoyed this book, **please** consider leaving a review, sharing on social media, and telling your reading friends.

THANK YOU!

GET THE NEXT BOOK...

The Keeper (Amish Country Brides)

Susan Miller is discontent with her Amish life, and resents the fact that her sisters' marriages have left her with all the hard work at home. Worse yet, annoying Josh Beachy shows up to help work on their farm, creating even more disruption. So she decides to do something drastic—leave the only life she's ever known. But when Susan finds herself in trouble, only then does she begin to rethink her choices.

When Joshua Beachy's family moves to a new Amish district in Indiana, he doesn't expect to meet "Spitfire" Susan Miller. He's never known a feisty Amish woman like her. While he admits that he finds her attractive, he knows the best course of action is to steer clear of her. And that's what he does, until she disappears one night.

Josh now feels compelled to watch after her, and insure no harm will befall her. But how can he keep her safe and maintain his good standing in the Amish community? Worse yet, how can he keep himself from falling in love with her?

Releasing September 7, 2021
PREORDER NOW

DISCUSSION QUESTIONS

1. Emily enjoys gardening and providing fresh fruit and vegetables for her family and community. Do you grow a garden? What are your favorite things to plant and harvest?

2. Do you believe in love at first sight? Why or why not?

3. Titus is interested in Emily, but he is shy. Are you shy?

4. Have you ever fostered orphaned kittens? Please share your experience.

5. Titus has a giving spirit and loves to spoil those he loves with gifts. Do you think his character is realistic for an Amish man?

6. Stemming for the previous question (which I've witnessed personally in an Amish friend's life), do you know of anyone like this?

7. Do you think ten years is too big of an age difference in a married couple? What's the largest age gap you would consider acceptable?

8. Titus discovered he enjoyed the men's fellowship. Do you meet with anyone for spiritual encouragement?

9. Sammy talks to Titus about being "knowing and being known of God." Do you have this kind of relationship with God?

10. Titus realizes that his life is controlled by fear. Do you have fears controlling your life? How can you utilize your faith to triumph over them?

A SPECIAL THANK YOU

I'd like to take this time to thank everyone that had any involvement in this book and its production, including my Mom and Dad, who have always been supportive of my writing, my longsuffering Family— especially my handsome, encouraging Hubby, my Amish and former-Amish friends who have helped immensely in my understanding of the Amish ways, my supportive Pastor and Church family, my Proofreaders, my Editor, my CIA Facebook author friends who have been a tremendous help, my wonderful Readers who buy, read, offer great input, and leave encouraging reviews and emails, my awesome Launch Team who, I'm confident, will 'Sprede the Word' about *The Teacher*! And last, but certainly not least, I'd like to thank my ***Precious LORD and SAVIOUR JESUS CHRIST***, for without Him, none of this would have been possible!

If you haven't joined my Facebook reader group, you may do so here:
https://www.facebook.com/groups/379193966104149/

Made in United States
Troutdale, OR
08/20/2024

22184654R00130